Secrets and Strangers

James Gilbert

ISBN: 0-6156-6932-8
ISBN-13: 9780615669328
Library of Congress Control Number: 2012944603
James\Gilbert
Silver Spring, MD

Part of the Amalfi series by James Cassell, the painting from which this cover borrows its image evokes the Mediterranean, where the first of the following stories takes place. All along the crescent-moon coast of Italy and Southern France, from Genoa to Nice, the mountains plunge directly into the translucent blue-green sea, shattering its reflections into a palette of stunning primary colors. Cassell's work captures the natural and man-made hues of limestone and volcanic rock, perched villages, and red-tiled roofs of this region, in a frame of chiaroscuro. Likewise, the themes of this book—secrets and strangers—deal with juxtapositions, ironies, unexpected revelations, and illuminations shaped by stark shadows.

Preface: The eleven stories collected here are arranged in no particular chronological order or by narrator or even subject but rather with regard to the power of place. The initial piece, from which the book takes its title, is set in Italy and is followed by two stories about Nice and then one in Prague. The next grouping shifts to a child's perspective in Illinois: first there are excursions into Southern Illinois and the musty pasts and misunderstandings it holds and then to Chicago. The next occur in Washington, DC, and the book ends with a story in Florida. None of the stories are true in the ordinary sense of that word, as any writer will stress about his or her work. But sometimes a simple phrase uttered, a brief, offhand remark made, demands the elaboration that only an imaginary plot and fictional characters can supply. Such accidental words and phrases are the stimulus for these stories and, I hope, convincing explanations of their meaning.

SECRETS AND STRANGERS

The Italian train felt slightly too warm and ripe with the smells of humans, cigarettes, and diesel fuel. With upright benches facing each other, the compartment was designed for conversation, or more: a casually touched knee, a gesture to seize attention. Or a large family passing food and drink across the small space that could become an imaginary table. But they were alone, facing each other, looking from opposite sides at the same landscape advancing and receding, making comments about the weather, catching glimpses of fields, villages, and water. Every few minutes the train twisted under another cutaway tunnel, with arches intermittently blocking the view of the lake, casting noisy shadows. These blackened structures flashed by, making the scenery sputter like an old-fashioned movie film that had jumped its sprockets.

Steve looked above her head at the luggage piled on the metal rack and then glanced to the door of the compartment. The curtain was half-drawn but still revealed the shape of an Italian man smoking a cigarette, crouched over to look out the corridor window, his hand dangling on the railing. Air from the open window rustled his black hair. He studied the figure a minute longer, but the man did not feel his intense stare.

"What do we do when we get there?" she asked.

"I've told you already. There's a short walk—at least it looks short on the map—down to the boat dock. We just find the right one. I'm sure I have enough lire. It should take only ten minutes or so over to the island."

"Maybe we should get a taxi from the train. The suitcases are pretty heavy."

"I can manage," he said.

"Well, of course you can, but it's kind of a vacation. Why not start it by relaxing a bit?"

"Not exactly a vacation, since I've brought so much work."

"But there will be time to meet other people, time to talk, time for us," she exclaimed, looking directly at him.

He turned away to look out the window again at the passing scenery: the narrow lake and the mountains jutting into it that held tiny pastel villages in their folds.

"You know you're not the friendliest person," she continued. "You'll need to try not to get too absorbed in your work. You can be selfish that way."

Of course she was right, and he needed her for that: to be right and to be friendly. But he could sense something else in her words: the suggestion of intimacy. He looked back at the Italian man in the corridor, who had scarcely shifted his body or his attention.

"Yes, I'll try," he replied, thinking of the month ahead and wondering what sort of effort it would require.

The train slowed as it entered a particularly long tunnel and was barely crawling when it emerged into Como. It stopped in what was obviously the upper part of the town because on three sides the walls of the mountain rose up like the background of an outdoor theater. Light from behind the station, in the town, and across the lake illuminated their arrival. Steve hoisted the two suitcases, and the couple stepped down from the car, crossed another set of tracks, and stopped in front of the station door. A large pot of red geraniums stood at either end of the metal canopy of the station. On the left, a patch of dark petunias exhaled a sweet perfume.

"I just want to get my bearings," he muttered as he put down the bags and pulled out a map provided by the Center. It showed a staircase at the front of the station that led down to a walkway along a stream and then, in about another hundred yards, to a small landing where they would find the boat launch. Several other passengers from the train passed by and walked around the edge of the station. They followed. Steve absently watched the Italian man as he stepped briefly into the arms of a woman with short hair that had been dyed auburn. The pair climbed into a large Fiat convertible and drove off.

He and Marilyn set out down the uneven stairs to the path beside the stream. Just as the map showed it, the road led, twisting, down uneven steps to the embarcadero. He bought their tickets with lire from a dirty roll of money he kept stuffed in his pocket, and then they joined the small group of passengers waiting for the ferry. A couple of them looked like Americans: a short, blond woman with blotched, angry skin and her fussy husband who appeared to think that his pacing would speed up the boat or deflect his wife's insistent chatter.

"The room is wonderful," she exclaimed. And he couldn't have agreed more. The tall French windows, covered with a billowy chintz curtain, looked out on a remarkable scene, a large garden dotted with huge, drooping red and pink roses. Beyond these beds lay a large sloping hill with olive trees and un-mown, dusty grass filled with wild flowers. The field ended at an old monastery that appeared to have once been painted a deep red but had now been bleached back to a dull cement color in streaks at the corners and around the foundation.

"I think I could get to like this place," Steve said as he focused on the por-tion of a path and a staircase visible in the panorama in front of him.

"So do I," she agreed. "So could we."

He held her eyes in his glance for a moment and then turned away, giving his attention back to his unpacking.

"I think I'll go to my office and set up the computer. Nothing like getting ready for work. Then, after dinner, I'll try to outline that first essay I have to write."

He was unsure why he felt the need to justify himself at this moment, to invent a schedule where none was needed. After all, it was a resident academic center, a month in the country just to consider his new theory about Thomas Cole's narrative paintings. Perhaps it was because he had reached the moment when he had almost formulated what he would say, that moment of lassitude and reluctance and foreboding—fear, even—that always preceded writing. Once he got started, however, he would speed through it, recklessly careen-ing through sentences, accelerating until he reached the end when the real task of writing—or rewriting—began. But he could never quite seem to avoid the enervation and anxiety that always struck right before he began.

"I'll meet you in the lounge at cocktail hour," he muttered, turning for the door.

"No, better, I'll come and get you. Shall I bring your jacket and tie?" she asked. "You'll need them."

"OK," Steve replied and then pushed outside and walked to the door of the adjacent office.

It was a spartan, scholarly room, furnished in no discernible style at all and dominated by a clear glass table. Atop it sat a computer and keyboard and, alongside, a neat pile of long white sheets of paper with one pen and one pencil. The arrangement looked like what it was: the official issue of implements for visiting scholars. The adjacent bookshelf was empty except for a tattered copy of an Italian–English dictionary, two or three Agatha Christie novels, and David Lodge's *Small World*. He pulled the novel off the shelf, opened it to the first page, and read its familiar disclaimer: If the events of the book seemed to resemble a certain famous scholar's center, it was nevertheless a wholly fictitious story. But no one who ever came here had any doubts that they were just like the cartoon characters satirized in the novel.

Steve sat on the stiff swivel chair and began to open the boxes that held the files, notes, and sketches that had been shipped ahead to the center. Arranging most of them on the edges of the table or on the bookshelf, he retrieved his own sketch of Cole's *Youth* from his great narrative series and placed it in the empty space he had made by moving the typing paper. He could never really write about art until he took a turn at sketching, in effect, tried to measure the distance between his own conception and the artist's. Whenever he failed to create a believable line, to reconstruct truthfully his rendering, indicated where the artist's genius prevailed and where the critic would be obliged to describe in prose what he could never render. His own, thin version of *Youth* was decidedly flat and secular, lacking the spiritual, brooding quality of the painting, and its gloom of intense faith. He glanced out the window. Certainly this remarkable setting had been used by painters over and over again, but the colors here were more subtle; there was more joy in the actual place. Above all, the Italian landscape bore no traces of Cole's Protestant anxiety. Here, beauty was sufficient. He was right to call his essay "The Sacralization of Nature." Did he mean, by that, he wondered, that Cole had moralized reality and made an illusion out of something beautiful and nothing more?

He continued to unpack until the room suddenly turned dark. He got up to turn on the light just as Marilyn tapped at the door. Together, they walked down the corridor to the antechamber of the dining room for drinks and an informal introduction to the other scholars.

They entered a large room animated by several conversations. A waiter dressed in a white coat and black pants stood in the middle pouring drinks. He smiled as they approached.

"A couple of scotch and waters," Steve told him. "If that's what you want, Marilyn."

"Well, no, actually, I want an aperitif," she said, "something bitter and Italian but not too strong."

"OK. I'll have the same." He ordered two Cinzanos.

They took their drinks and turned to consider which of the conversations to join. Almost immediately the American couple from the boat came over. They both seemed more relaxed now, and he held out his hand.

"I'm John Devoto, from Kent State, and this is my wife, Cindy Belmont. She teaches American Studies at Cleveland. I'm a biologist."

They introduced themselves, and Cindy quickly said to him, "I know your work. Aren't you supposed to be writing a book on Thomas Cole? I have a student who says he's an admirer of yours."

Steve introduced Marilyn and then studied John's face more closely. There was something familiar in it.

"Do you by any chance know Vincent Devoto?" he said. "Is he possibly a relative? The last time I saw him, he was still in Florida somewhere. It must have been some convention."

"Actually, he's my brother. You're right; he teaches at the University of Florida. I'll have to tell him we met the next time I see him."

Steve looked at John again. He was the fortunate sibling. He was slender, dark, and almost handsome, except for his wide, bleary eyes. Just then a tall bearded man approached.

"Hello and welcome," he exclaimed to all four of them. "I've been here the longest, so I consider myself a welcoming committee of one. But...I'm leaving in a couple of days, rotating out! My name is Bingham, George Bingham. I do economics in New York."

Steve recognized him. Bingham was well-known as a newspaper columnist and an occasional guest on one of the minor Sunday-morning political shows. But he also knew his wife, Liz, who had been his classmate at awhile in 1965. When he told him, Bingham laughed loudly and gestured to include everyone in the room.

"*Small world*, you know. David Lodge's book. What a wonderful idea for a novel. Really skewered us all, don't you think? They must put a copy of his novel in every office, just to warn you of what's coming. It's like the Gideon Bible for scholars. You can't hide in a place like this. Everyone knows you or, worse, knows someone who knows something about you. There aren't any secrets here."

Steve laughed and looked into his eyes and then at Marilyn. He noted that, off to the side, the waiter was packing up the drinks wagon. He was short and verging on being stocky. In five years, he probably wouldn't notice him, but now…he smiled and then turned away.

"Time to go in," exclaimed Bingham, and they meandered into the dining room. Without designated places, everyone hesitated at first. It was a lovely, cool room with two long tables neatly laid out with heavy white tablecloths, napkins, and silver. Carafes of wine stood at either end. They sat down, Marilyn on his right and Bingham at the head. He hastily introduced them to everyone else at the table and then poured himself a glass of wine.

"OK, now," he exclaimed. "Let's get down to it and find out who you know."

He was eerily right. As the evening passed, it became clear that, between Marilyn and Steve, they could establish some personal link to almost half the other scholars, even the non-Americans. It was a small world indeed where even less than six degrees of separation was the norm.

Despite the academic chatter, the meal passed quickly. One dish followed another, deftly served by two waiters, one of whom had poured their drinks. He managed to learn his name, Gino. As he watched him clear the table, he was vaguely aware that Marilyn was following his stare. Perhaps he would keep his looks for more than five years after all.

After dinner, they returned to the antechamber for more drinks and then went to their room. "I'll just look in on my chapter," Steve said to Marilyn. "You go ahead and go to bed. I'll be back in an hour or so." She agreed, and when he returned, he found her half-dozing, her novel flopped onto the floor. He picked it up and dog-eared her place. Then he turned out the light. After undressing, he climbed into bed and watched the occasional ruffle of curtains and listened to a staccato chorus of Italian crickets.

And so they spent the next two weeks with work punctuated by splendid meals, conversation, and a few side trips to Milan and Lake Lugano. He could sense, however, that Marilyn, much as she liked her own routine of reading, walking, and taking short shopping trips to town, was looking forward to her upcoming trip to Assisi where friends were spending the week.

On the morning of her departure, they rose early. Steve watched as she carefully placed four days' clothing into a small bag. Her gestures were almost needlessly efficient, as she found the perfect spot for each item. She knew where everything fit—just like with their lives—and packed days up like in a suitcase for a well-planned itinerary. The early-morning sun poured into the room and lit two spots on the amber ceramic floor beneath the windows. The reflection warmed her face, which he studied as she continued her work. In this light she looked young, her wide brown eyes concentrating on her task. Marilyn always had a somewhat surprised look on her face, a physiognomy that charmed strangers who could not believe at first in the contrast between this opening, inviting look and the frugality and bluntness of her conversation. He noticed, in the light, the traces of her makeup. It was heavy but expertly done, with clever shadowing and contrasting bright spots.

"Will you be all right? I'll be gone for four days," she said, holding her tickets in hand and looking for the proper compartment to place them in.

"Sure," Steve responded, "I have my chapter. I've reached the point I told you about—where I have to formulate the argument. Then I can finish it. I'll probably be done when you get back."

"Yes," she said. "That's why I asked. You always have trouble somewhere in the stretch. But I just meant would you promise not to be unsociable? Don't sink into self-indulgence. The writing isn't everything."

"You know I can get along without you," he said without exactly understanding what he meant. "In fact, I like being alone: sometimes I work better."

"True," she smiled. "But you get to be so antisocial; you retreat into yourself when I'm gone."

Her words caused neither a twinge of anger nor embarrassment. Steve let them pass and thought, for a moment, about all the other times he had been alone. It brought on the anticipation of freedom, memories of brief moments of self-indulgence and desire. Yes, he usually retreated but not into himself so much as into another self, where being alone meant the possibility of another identity. Like in the anonymity of a strange city or an airport waiting zone where no face was familiar, where it was possible to imagine being anyone for a moment, even one's own true self.

"That's why you're here," Steve said finally. "To keep me on the straight and narrow. No, that's unkind…To keep me living the life I've chosen. To make it all work."

She looked up at him and then turned back to close the suitcase. He walked over to the bed and picked up the valise by the handle.

"Let's go on down now," she said. "The taxi will be here any minute now. Gino promised to call one for me." In their three weeks, she had begun an amusing acquaintance with the stocky waiter, server of drinks, and general handyman at the Center. She had, in fact, stepped into an easy familiarity and bantering intimacy that was not possible for him.

They walked to the front entrance of the Center.

"I could have walked you down to the boat. A taxi isn't really necessary," he said futilely.

"No. It's my trip. I like the convenience." She turned and smiled purposefully as if she had practiced the words that were to come. "Promise me you won't avoid the others. Stay for drinks after dinner. You know, not everything is work."

"OK." He nodded. "Anyway, there's a new group of scholars coming in tonight. Finally, that artist...what's his name...will be here. I won't mind meeting him."

As the taxi drove up, its tires crunched on the gravel of the circular driveway. It was black, official-looking, and very clean. The driver jumped out and extended his hand for the baggage. Marilyn turned and embraced him lightly. Their cheeks touched, leaving a dusting of her familiar face powder and perfume on his. Then she bent and climbed through the open back door of the car. The driver carefully closed it, rushed around to the front, and began to pull away. Marilyn smiled and waved, although he didn't know whether she was happy to be underway, thinking of him, or just amused at the officious haste of the driver.

Late that afternoon, Steve returned from the office to their room to change for drinks and dinner. He hadn't managed a word or, rather, all the words he had written had to be deleted from the chapter. He simply hadn't been able to write what he felt about Cole. The thoughts were inside him, but they refused to push through the passage he prepared for them. Was it, he had been wondering, a lifetime of repressing emotion that made simple sentences so difficult to shape? Had he succeeded too well in burying deep in his psyche the thoughts that should have been obvious and natural to him? Perhaps, he thought, he would take the day off tomorrow and wander around Lake Como. It would be refreshing just to watch life from a cafe, to imagine himself undefined by anything except that present moment and an anonymous place.

8

He strode into the dining room antechamber late. Drinks were almost over. Two or three clusters of scholars stood around in familiar groups. He hesitated before joining one where the Devotos were chatting animatedly with the person who must have been the newest arrival. "Come and meet Bill Hendley," Cindy said, guiding him into the circle.

"Very happy to meet you," he said somewhat distractedly. He was about Steve's height but balding and heavyset. He was also too old, he thought, to be wearing a small emerald-colored stone in his left ear. He took his hand warmly.

"Actually," he said, "it's not 'how do you do?' but 'how are you after all these years?' I expect you don't recognize me yet?"

Steve looked more carefully, but he could not penetrate the disguise of so many years.

"You know, Bill Hendley from Brown. We knew each other briefly in undergraduate art history. I used to sit next to you."

Then, he remembered. He looked carefully again, using his imagination to sculpt away the years, smooth the lines, and discard the extra weight. His confused emotions roared, and he felt a churn of embarrassment, as if he had suddenly been caught. His hands and face suddenly seemed hot and dry.

"Yes," Steve responded. "We did know each other once. I had completely forgotten about that class."

"But you couldn't have forgotten me."

"Well, almost, but no. Of course I haven't forgotten you," he confessed.

"That's just like the Center," said Cindy. "It brings people together again. The past doubles in upon itself. Small world."

"I understand you're married," Bill said. "Where's your wife? Did she come with you?"

Something about the question sounded threatening, and he forced himself to be civil in replying. He wondered if the effort showed. "She's off with friends seeing the Italian countryside. She'll be back Friday night."

"Well, I can't wait to meet her. I'm curious about the sort of woman you would marry—who would marry you. And there's lots I can tell her about the good old days at Brown. Things she'd never imagine."

"And you've become a painter; am I right?" Steve said somewhat too loudly. "Funny. I haven't heard much about you." His unkind remark startled the group, which began to look anxiously at the dining room door, as if willing it to open.

"Well, I do work mostly around the Cincinnati area. Some experiments in art education, some installations, and some collage pieces. Not the sort of work you'd find in a New York gallery. Why don't you come down to the studio tomorrow morning and I'll show you? By then I should be set up."

"OK," he muttered, and as the doors opened, he pushed into the dining room, riding a wave of anxiety.

The following morning, gloom had settled over the lake, and the mountains had disappeared behind a curtain of mist. The grass, olive trees, and paths looked like they had been splattered with grease. A cool wind whipped around the buildings and banged a door left open somewhere in the Center. He wasn't hungry but choked down part of a croissant and orange marmalade. Even the coffee tasted stale and diluted.

After breakfast, he went back to his office and turned on the computer. The screen was the only light in the room. He called up the file, Cole.10, and read the opening lines. "Shit," he muttered, "I ought to erase the whole mess." He could not get to the center of the book yet, with or without solitude. In fact, he hadn't written a word since Marilyn left, at least not any he could keep, and she was due back in a couple of days. He got up and swallowed hard. He had to see Bill now: he would be able to straighten him out. No more innuendos, no hints, no pressure. He couldn't stand that in this crowd of strangers who knew him so well.

He left the office and returned to the room. He put on the new red and blue Italian sweater he had bought, combed his hair, and carefully brushed his teeth, angry all the while at himself for caring about his appearance. He glanced into the mirror and saw a confused face defined by age, compromise, and deflected desire. His heart pounded as he went down the staircase and across the stone pavement to Bill's basement studio. He knocked sharply, and Bill opened the door quickly, as if he had been hovering near it.

The room was brightly lit by a line of windows across the top of one wall and by several strong lamps and spotlights. The latter had been carefully aimed at a couple of incomplete collages and several easels on which Bill had placed designs for installations. He was surprised to find the beginning of an oil landscape set up in the middle of the room.

"I couldn't help it," he said. "Coming in last evening was so amazing. I've never seen any scene as perfectly framed. It's almost as if you lose consciousness of anything but the focal point, the perspective. And I've never seen such exquisite colors and black shadows. So I'm painting again. The sort of thing I used to do back at Brown."

"Yes, Brown," Steve said. "Look...all of that is very much in the past. Let's just put that aside. I'm sorry I was brusque last night, but you worried me and so suddenly."

"You of all people ought to know that the past can't ever be over," he replied. "You live in it. You've made it your whole world. You imagine yourself back there sometimes in the nineteenth century when there wasn't even a vocabulary to describe what you are. Why can't you just relax and admit it?"

"And what's that?" Steve broke in. "What's that? How do you know what I am?"

"Well, maybe you don't know, maybe your wife doesn't know, maybe the scholars here don't know...but I do. And I'm not embarrassed about who I am; why should you be?"

Steve was furious. He knew where this was heading: a public confession and execution; he could see the instruments of torture.

"Gather round and listen to me destroy my life, everyone," he blurted out angrily. "Let me tell you about years of compromise, count the building blocks in my edifice of deceit, help me bring down the whole structure in an earthquake of blunt shocks."

"Don't be sarcastic...that's just your way of retreating from the truth. Look, you're extraordinarily uptight. I can see it easily; so can everyone else. You know why."

"Yes, I know why. It's about choices I've made. None of which have anything to do with you," he retorted. "You've been out of my life for twenty years. Now stay out!"

"But I can't. I'm in your life. Being open about who I am has been a terrific struggle. I've suffered for everyone...for you even. You have no right to keep quiet," he said firmly.

Steve looked him straight in the eyes. He could see both what attracted him and what repelled him back then during their short affair. He hated him and his threat: he wanted to escape the room—but at the same time he wanted to linger long enough to inflict some sort of hurt.

Bill seemed to read his thoughts, and he stepped forward with an intensity generated by his whole body. Steve put out his hand and pulled him close. For a moment they stood in a loathing embrace. And then, Steve felt, just as suddenly, the sting of remembrance. His body was taut, and his mouth was on his so suddenly and harshly that their teeth cracked. Steve pushed his tongue between his lips and enveloped him, pressing him close as if to totally absorb and surround him. They held each other for a minute, and then Bill pushed away.

"You bastard," Bill exclaimed. "That's not what I meant. How could you think I want you? That—the desire—is all over, if I ever did desire you. I just wanted you to know the truth. What we did twenty years ago means nothing to me now and meant nothing to me then. Look, you even forgot it. But you still are what you are, despite your careful life and your careful, boring scholarship. Just remember what I know and that because of that, you will always know. Now take off. And don't worry; I can be private if I want to. Besides, I have my eye on that waiter. You probably noticed him, too. Why should I waste efforts on you?"

Steve looked at him for a long, tense moment and then glanced around the room.

Suddenly relieved, he replied, "Maybe you'll let me see the progress of your landscape from time to time. It's a problem I'm working on myself. You could be of help." He turned before Bill could say anything and walked out of the studio and into the misty daylight.

Marilyn came home the next night bearing small, cellophane envelopes of carefully chosen postcards, two or three silk scarves, a tie for him, and gossip about their friends.

"Assisi was wonderful. But the Whalens aren't in good shape. They bicker endlessly about their children, but I think it's just misplaced hostility. You know they've never worked out why they married each other? It was probably passion, certainly, at first, until it faded. But longtime partnerships aren't easy to achieve, and that's what matters, doesn't it?"

"Well, ours is solid," Steve said.

She smiled and looked carefully at him.

"Did you finish your chapter? Did you meet the new artist? What is he like? Did anything happen while I was gone?"

He knew she presented her questions in the exact opposite order of her concern. It was a habit of hers that he loved, although he never quite knew how to answer her.

"No, nothing happened," he said, taking a quiet breath. "Except that the artist who arrived is Bill Henley, someone I knew vaguely in college. And, no, I didn't make much progress on the chapter, but I think I might solve it now."

She smiled again and then looked away and said softly, almost inaudibly "So there still can be secrets."

DINNER UNDER A
STRIPED AWNING

The restaurant wrapped around the corner of the Boulevard Gambetta and the Avenue Victor Hugo, which it joined at a sixty-degree angle. I had strolled by the Le Coin Enfleuri several times before to look at the menu and to consider if this would be the place. It had an accommodating look; its tables were set back from the street and sheltered by a striped awning on one side and a large plane tree on the boulevard. The principle virtue was its location away from the torrents of crowds damming up the downtown: tall, emaciated Germans, pink, fat Americans looking for bargains, and parades of French tourists with their diminutive, white, fluffy dogs trotting briskly along with them. The flower market, the port, and the long pedestrian mall were all about the same in terms of their uninteresting tourist fare. In the old town, it was possible to find authentic Niçoise food in the tiny restaurants that spilled onto the broad steps that ran up and down the side streets. There was also what was out of the question: the really elegant restaurants along the Promenade des Anglais, facing the Mediterranean. No, the neighborhood place was clearly the best, and it had the virtue of being only a few blocks from the hotel.

I nodded to the waiter, and his hand gestured toward the empty tables, inviting me to choose one. It was early—indeed, I was the first client to arrive. I chose a position near the front window of the restaurant, under the awning and away from the traffic, and sat down. The waiter came over immediately with a menu and started to take away the paper place setting, plate, and silver opposite me. I gestured for him to stop and then ordered a beer. I would wait for my companion, I told him.

The street was still crowded with shoppers carrying baguettes and plastic bags from the nearby grocery store, which I could see just across the street. A line from the next-door boulangerie, advertising itself as *a l'ancienne*, extended out onto the sidewalk. Slightly further down, a man was pulling the metal shutters over the front of his tiny hardware storefront. Even from here, I could hear the dry rattle of the aluminum slats as they plunged down to cover the display window and door. Most of the stores closed between half past seven and eight, but the restaurant was still almost deserted. It would begin to fill in an hour or so. The waiter brought my beer and placed it carefully on a round cork coaster to prevent the moisture from seeping into the red Provençal tablecloth. I took a deep drink, sat back, and turned to watch the pedestrian traffic. This was a constant pleasure to me. There was something uninhibited, even aggressive, about street life in Nice. Not, of course, that everyone was transparent. Far from it. But no one seemed to be confined at home: not the too fat, the ugly, the deformed, or the beautiful—all participated in this daily parade. They all walked with the same presence, as if, I thought, they took pride in the role they had been selected to play, no matter its difficulty or inconsequence. It was their allotment. It was also my role to watch; that came with the price of the dinner.

Much of the foot traffic consisted of elderly women, often diminutive and sometimes hunched over by the weight of their packages. They entered and exited slowly and carefully from the buses running up and down the street. Strangely, I thought, many of them seemed to know one another and immediately started chatting when they confronted one another, avoiding the elaborate three kisses on both cheeks that younger people engaged in when greeting each other in public. I often wondered about these women. Did they live alone? Had they retired to Nice to nurse their elderly partners and then, to their surprise and anguish, live well beyond them and be really alone for the first times in their lives? Were their days divided into rituals of shopping, eating, cleaning, and watching television with a moment for passing gossip? French television, its celebrations of intelligence and of youth, of elegance, and of fashion and its serious pretensions and meandering discussions, would probably offer them nothing. Did they watch the game shows that promised to fulfill some contestant's dreams of money and adventure? Was there any room for them in this cruel array of impossible aspirations?

I looked around for Clare. She wasn't late by any means, although I wouldn't have been surprised if this ended up being the case. I didn't expect her for a half hour or so. I glimpsed a strange couple that passed in front me: a middle-aged and a younger man. They appeared quite ordinary until I focused on the oddity of the son (I presumed). They walked slowly, matching their gait to the other foot traffic. I had the sense that the father was guiding his compan-

16

ion, urging him on, issuing silent commands with a gentle touch to the elbow. The son seized my attention. His profile seemed unnaturally flat, as if it were a two-dimensional drawing. He had surprisingly black hair and whitish skin. His nose zigzagged along the plane of his face at an acute angle. His mouth fell into an almost chinless recess. When he turned toward me, at some word from his father, he revealed his astonishing thinness: a head that seemed to lack sides so that his features only made a profile, like a sheet of cutout paper.

Father and son continued walking slowly and purposefully down the boulevard. It was not cruelty but instinct that made me speculate about the son. There was the defect of his face that kept him tethered to his father. But nothing, it appeared, could prevent their evening stroll. I had seen a small bus (with *Service Sociale de Nice* stenciled on the side) somewhat earlier in the day. It stopped to pick up a passenger at an apartment building near the hotel. Perhaps the boy spent the day in some sort of center and then returned home for the evening, his stroll, and a silent dinner with his bewildered and anxious parents. I watched as another couple approached the restaurant. They appeared to know the waiter, who greeted them effusively and watched them choose a table on the main sidewalk, in the center and in full view of the passing foot traffic. They were a youngish pair of thirty years or so, with fading good looks and elegant, tanned skin. The woman was bronze-colored, with a brilliant red dye in her hair. She was wearing a simple dress of burnt orange blocked with yellow sunflowers. Her jewelry consisted of two heavy gold chains and matching bracelets that self-consciously set off her skin color. But her face had already begun to show the damage of the sun, which had burned abrasions and roughness into its surface. Soon it would erupt into a mortal battlefield of lines and trenches. And yet women like this crowded the beaches from midday through afternoon, allowing the heat and sun to corrode their youth in exchange for the luminous deposit it left on their skin. Her companion had striking good looks: jet-black hair set against nut-brown skin, which I suspected was pretty much his natural color. He was wearing a soft-blue, open-collared, short-sleeved shirt that fell perfectly around his slightly rounded shoulders and chest. His pants were taupe and tight-fitting. He had on white loafers with no socks. Like most French men, he wore jewelry: a very thin gold necklace and a large, silver ring on his right hand. He carried a black leather purse, which he deposited on the table.

When the waiter returned with two menus, the couple ordered an aperitif: something yellow in tall glasses with ice. They both reached for cigarettes almost simultaneously. He offered his lighter, and they both inhaled and looked around. First, they glanced at me (an insufficient audience), and then, expectantly, they turned their attention to the passing foot traffic. They settled in for an evening of watching and being admired. I could see that they had little to say to each other: half a sentence here and there, some muffled comment about a pedestrian, and later, an evaluation of the food.

Clare appeared suddenly, breaking into the fictions I was designing for the passing pedestrians and my dinner companions.

"I'm sorry. Am I late?" she said breathlessly, slipping into her chair and sliding a plastic shopping bag under the table. "Just a few things I couldn't pass up on. You know, Richard, the sales are amazing. You ought to buy yourself something. French clothes look good on you."

Clare beamed when she talked, her face animated with excitement for the ambience, the wonderful, now-fading blue sky that tinted every object in its long rays a gentle pink, the food...me. I could feel the warmth of her affection radiating from her smile, carried along by an intimate stare. There was no doubting it: Clare was a beautiful woman. She attracted the discreet approval of many of the women who passed her by and the sometimes exaggerated stares of young men. Without looking at all French, without their slim, tailored good looks and aggressively made-up faces, she nonetheless managed a natural sophistication. Perhaps it was her short, straight hair, cut just below her ears, or her luminous, pale skin, or perhaps it was just the ensemble: the way she walked, glanced around herself with appreciation and grace, and greeted most situations with a muted, bell-like laugh.

"I probably shouldn't have. It's so clichéd, but I bought a tablecloth of Provençal material—almost like this one but nicer—and a pair of very high heels. Something for the apartment; something for me. And it's such fun shopping. The old town just reeks of lavender and perfumed soaps and spices. I wonder I don't smell of it myself. I stopped for a coffee in front of the Palais de Justice. It's such fun to see the lawyers—I guessed that's what they were—racing across the square in their cutoff black robes, tails flying, and singularly unprofessional and young-looking. Somehow it doesn't seem serious here and more like the set of a comic opera..." Clare stopped her enthusiastic monologue abruptly. "And how about you? Did you get to the bank? Do we have the rental car?"

Before I could answer, the waiter appeared with another menu. Clare took it, placed it absently on the table, and glanced at the chalkboard list of daily specials on the wall to the left. "Oh, I'll have the *dorade* in tarragon sauce. And a good wine, don't you think, Richard? To celebrate."

I loved the way she took command—took possession—with such ease and elegance. "Sure," I replied, turning to the waiter. "The white Burgundy. I'll have the salmon. And a salad for each of us." The waiter marked his pad, tore off the top sheet and placed it on our table under a small marble weight, and retreated.

"It's really wonderful to be here," Clare resumed. "Thanks so much for inviting me along, that is, to join you. What a splendid idea it is for you to come to France every summer. You must eventually feel part of the life here. And I suppose you've made some friends by now?" This last was as much a question as an assertion; perhaps she wanted me to tell her.

"Yes, I've met some people," I replied, edging close to a subject I preferred to leave unmentioned for the moment.

"Well, someday I'd like to meet..." she said, trailing off into another thought. She had the habit of racing from one subject to the next, sometimes only revealing a glimpse of what was turning over in her mind. On occasion, it could be infuriating, but sometimes it was charming, particularly when I could conjure the trigger that made her skip to something new: an image, someone passing by, a noise. Sometimes she would even tell me.

"I hope you don't mind, but I'd like to go to Biot and then on to Vallauris tomorrow. I've seen some pottery in shop windows here, but I imagine it's better at the source where they make it. I've been reading in the guidebook about all the potters in those two towns. We could get up early, miss most of the traffic, and have lunch there...Oh, I'm sorry. I'm planning your day for you. But I was just noticing the pattern on the tablecloth, and it reminded me."

"No, no, not at all. Let's go tomorrow. I'm delighted when you plan things. It's your way of being happy. It's the slow and thoughtful moments I'll be wary of. So, if we get on the road by nine o'clock, miss the rush hour, and beat the shoppers, we'll find parking, and you can browse until lunch. Is this for your collection? Do you have something special in mind?"

"No," she said, "I just want an occasional piece...a vase, perhaps, or some plates or even a few tiles for the kitchen. There's something so energetic about Provençal colors. They seem so bright and pure and deep. Matisse and the others—they were just painting what they saw, making art of the humdrum vision that peasants see a hundred times a day. What I really want and can't have," she said dreamily, "is an old stone wall and a small arched cutout for a pot of red geraniums."

"You could have it in a painting or a photograph," I offered.

"Oh, yes," she said, "a painting or a photograph. But wouldn't it be wonderful to live behind that wall, to see it every time you went in or out of the house, especially in the morning or evening when the sun comes in at a sharp angle, just catching and exploding the red against the wall? A color like that is almost audible."

Clare wasn't so much dramatic as she was a scene-maker, an inventor of life and someone who could sketch a picture in her mind's eye and then fill it with people: herself and her friends and always me. It enticed her to plan, to anticipate being somewhere else, somewhere romantic or exciting. I had often wondered why such a beautiful woman needed such an escape, if it was an escape, although perhaps it wasn't really about being somewhere or someone else but a way of heightening reality. She was really an artist in a sense in that she imagined the perfect setting and then placed herself at the center of it. I wondered if there was a degree...no...a strong element of self-deception in all this. For example, her attitude toward me—why did she persist when she could have had so many lovers? Perhaps it was the challenge of my personal scenery and a lifestyle she couldn't enter into completely, couldn't even imagine.

"I think you would tire of it, don't you?" I said. "Beauty will only take you so far. And then, after that, there's boredom or work or long plane trips and long lines at customs."

"But you don't seem to mind," she shot back. "You manage to suffer through all the inconveniences every year. And when you're here, doesn't the unpleasantness of the trip disappear—fade in the bright sun and blue skies?"

"Yes, of course, you're right," I said, and I wondered if that wasn't the attraction between us, our ability to imagine, to endure all sorts of unpleasantness for the sake of a moment, a splendid view, a table placed just right in a restaurant, food that smelled and tasted of the flowers and herbs that grew here. We were both dreamers, to be sure, daydreamers of a special sort who could impose their desires on reality and see, like with the zoom of a camera, only that portion of exaggerated reality they allowed into their focus.

20

The waiter burst out of the kitchen with a small flourish, carrying two plates and a large salad bowl. He placed them quickly on the table and returned a minute later with the wine.

"Shall I pour, monsieur?" he asked.

"No, it's fine as it is," I replied. I reached over and splashed the cold wine into our glasses. "Well, to Nice," I said, raising mine.

"To us in Nice," Clare responded. Taking a quick bite of her fish, she exclaimed, "My dinner; it's wonderful. How is yours?"

"The same," I replied. Glancing around, I became aware that the restaurant was almost full now: a sudden rush of customers had entered, as if they all came at an appointed hour. Most were couples, with an odd single skewing the mix here and there. Since there was only one waiter, whom I imagined to be the owner, with his wife in the kitchen, it would be slow from now on, as people ordered portions of their meals and then considered whether to try something else. "Life à la carte," I laughed to myself. And I knew that we would have to work diligently to catch the waiter's attention for our bill. It was always like that: you could order, and you could eat, but you could never leave a French restaurant.

"What's so amusing?" Clare broke in. "You have a delicious smile on your face. Some sort of joke?"

"Oh," I said, leaning back in my chair and putting down my knife and fork. "You remember what I always say about French restaurants?"

"Yes, I do."

"It always happens."

"But I like it; it's one of the pleasures of being here…not to be rushed and bullied or reminded of the mundane," she said and paused. "You know, you don't have to tell me about your life here. I can see you're being evasive. I don't ever have to know the details." Clare never looked lovelier than when she was curious and puzzled, her face poised for enlightenment.

"I'll tell you if you really want to know," I replied.

Despite having prepared for this moment, I still found it difficult to begin.

"I've always known," Clare said encouragingly. "Not the details, of course. But we've been so close for so long. I couldn't not know, could I?"

"Well, I have a couple of friends I see regularly. I suppose you can imagine where I met them. They're both married. I…we…prefer it that way since there are no strings and no regrets. It's one of the reasons—not the only one—that I

21

come here. It keeps me from having to commit myself in my real life. Am I telling you too much already? Living here for a month or so every summer gives me a chance to masquerade as another person, where no one knows me, where I'm even a stranger to myself. That seems to work so that when I go back, there's no less confusion about life but at least a kind of temporary quiet."

"I do understand," Clare interrupted. "Not that you're asking for understanding. My eyes are wide open."

That was the least truth Clare could have said about herself. She never accepted reality for what it was. She always embellished and changed it to suit herself. But, still, I did know what she meant and, I thought, perhaps even why she said it.

"So, Richard, the point is that I want to get married," she continued, looking straight into my eyes. "We have a wonderful relationship. We have fun together. We love each other...and I think it's a splendid idea to marry your best friend. That would make it permanent."

"You would do that, knowing what you know? That I will always... wouldn't ever give up my other self...never really share one hundred percent?"

"My God," she exclaimed, "what couple gives anything like that much of themselves?. Or would want to? No, I certainly don't claim all of you. And you certainly wouldn't want in on all my daydreams."

"Oh, you reveal those in spite of yourself," I said. "It's part of what makes you so charming...the telltale traces of your imagination, your stage settings. Would you want children?"

"Certainly, and so would you. You'll make a wonderful father."

Just at that moment, the waiter appeared. "Do you desire dessert...a coffee?" he asked in the rushed formal manner that suggested he was at the hard-pressed height of his duty.

"Two coffees," Clare ordered. "OK, Richard?"

I nodded yes, and the waiter rushed off. Almost immediately I could hear, from behind the bar, the clatter of small china cups and the hiss of the cappuccino machine. Most of the other tables had by now been served with either a main course or at least an appetizer, and the food and drink animated conversation. The ambient noise grew louder, and a wave of cigarette smoke swept over us as the first patrons finished one course and used the interlude to smoke.

"I do love you, Clare. And you're right about the children. It would be wonderful to bring them here...to let them see...to have them grow up sharing our joy in such places. But beyond that, I couldn't promise you…Is that really enough for you? You're a beautiful woman. You could have had—could have almost anyone and completely."

"The problem with those one-hundred-percent fellows you mentioned," she laughed, "is that they turn into boring…I don't know what. I think they lack something fundamental."

"A feminine sensibility?" I interjected.

"No, not quite that, Richard, and don't make light of it. More like the ability to dream. They accept things as they are instead of insisting they be as you want them to be. Life without illusions is empty and ordinary. What should I do? Marry some hulk of a man who wants to watch football all Sunday, who grunts instead of speaks?"

"That's not your only choice, Clare," I said. "The world isn't divided so starkly and dramatically that way."

"I think you're wrong, Richard. Oh, it wouldn't seem so at first. But after a few years, most men grow into themselves, which would mean away from me, and toward their work and sports. They become passive observers; they never really become participants in their own lives—let alone in mine. I'm very demanding, you know. I think the only time you see couples really equal, where they understand each other, is when they are old: at the androgynous end of life. And I don't want to wait for that, don't want it ever…after most of the energy is gone away, and we are wearing matching pastel shades of green and pink and dreaming of a condo in Miami. No, I want life now and you now and in the most intense Provençal colors!"

Clare could be stubborn and very convincing. "I certainly share that vision with you Clare," I said, "and I do love you in my way. If you want to get married, to have children, to share our visions, I would like that more than anything. It's just that I want you to understand the limitations."

"Oh, I do," she shot back. "It will be perfect; you'll see, Richard. Just like…you remember the story I told you about Elsa Lancaster and Charles Laughton or Linda and Cole Porter? Not to push the analogy too far, after all, but, my God, they managed to stage wonderful, beautiful lives together. And so could we even without being British or movie stars or songwriters."

"All right, Clare, let's take the chance. We can be ourselves or whomever else you'd like to imagine. We have talked about this before and agreed before. So let's create that life together, now."

The waiter arrived with our coffees, and I took a sugar lump from the silver bowl in the middle of the table, broke it in the palm of my hand, and dropped half into my cup.

"Do you want the other half?" I asked.

"Oh, yes," beamed Clare, laughing at the symbolism. "I accept."

"Then, are you ready to go back to the hotel?" I asked.

"Well, I will be in about twenty minutes. I just want to savor the moment."

"Good," I said, breaking out into a laugh at my own joke. "Then I'll start trying to get the bill from the waiter."

THE CHERRY TREES

It rained occasionally during the long winter in Nice, although not enough to be memorable. But the wind whipped frequently around our house, swirling up along the contours of the hilltop, defining our days. Sometimes it held a bank of motionless, low-hanging clouds along the coast, never pushing them quite inland over the margin of the sea, or else it blew the sky cold and clear as the mistral raced from the Arctic Circle to the Sahara. Once in a while, it probed and shook the loose shutters on the north wall of the house, and in the front it snagged itself in the fronds of the solitary palm tree, pulling them taut as if untangling a child's hair.

The house itself was immense, empty, and cold and yet cluttered with pieces of broken and sad furniture, piles of books, and half-finished paintings leaning against the wall. There were three bedrooms, although we only occupied two, and a large, bright studio that opened onto a balcony, a view of the front garden, and finally the Mediterranean. The surrounding garden itself had passed into an unkempt field of weeds and a few sickly, bright flowers poking their bright heads above the tall brown grass. We were told that it had once been a carnation farm.

Dominated by a large worktable blotted with spills of oil paint and covered with empty tubes, the studio showed the same disorder with randomly placed tools and boxes of brushes. I could imagine M. Martin squeezing the last oily spurt onto one of the smeared pallets that leaned against the wall and then discarding the spent tube in the corner. From the looks of it, he must have shoveled the color in globs onto the canvas. What remained of his work were seven or eight unfinished abstracts, mostly in earth and yellow tones. We often joked about the absentminded abstractionist too distracted to finish a single work.

We met M. Martin in the fall, shortly after we arrived in Nice. I advertised for a flat in the *Nice Matin*, and his phone call in response led us up a winding country road to the top of the western-most of the three immense hills rising out of the city. M. Martin was a small and fussy man who directed us to park in a precise spot at the end of the long gravel driveway. Following the dance of his arms, we stopped and got out into the bright autumn light. It was a strange and impressionable view: the vast panorama of the Mediterranean in the distance and the ruined and desiccated fields surrounding the house. M. Martin extended a mitt of fat fingers, and we touched in a brief, formal, up-and-down, French handshake. He turned to my wife, nodded slightly, and took her hand in turn.

"Emily," I said.

"And who is this?" he asked in English that was so accented that I thought at first it might be French.

"This is Jeremy." And Jeremy put out his hand with the boldness of a child who has not yet learned to be shy.

"This is the house," he indicated, pirouetting on his heel. It was a large, three-story peasant cottage with a front terrace giving off to the living room, a dark entryway beneath it, and a huge bougainvillea that twisted up a support column and then spread across the railing of the terrace, a dusty mass of dying blossoms in the fall season now a passionless ruin. Some of its magenta-purple flowers were still brilliant in the midday sun and seemed to clash with every other color of the landscape. The puzzle was their absolute lack of scent—there was not even the vague, humid presence that other odorless flowers sometimes exude. It was something that made me vaguely uncomfortable and, over the course of the winter and spring, I would wonder again and again how a plant so beautiful could be so sterile and why its breeders had been so negligent of other joys, as if its beauty were forced in a solitary, heroic effort that left it exhausted and depleted of all other senses.

M. Martin invited us in to the ground floor of storerooms and then led us up a long staircase to the main floor. On this level were a large living room, a dining room, and a kitchen, with a water closet in the hallway. None of the furnishings quite matched. Any ancient ensembles that might have once existed had gradually lost pieces until they merged into the general disorder. The kitchen was filled with shelves of glasses and plates from two or three different sets and drawers brimming with knives and forks, pots and pans, and cooking tools. The stove was an ancient, black gas range that required a match to light or a mechanical flint wand that shot a spark out the end. It was clean but had an untidy air.

Throughout the first level, the floor was covered with loose red clay tiles that crunched and clattered as we stepped across them. The only artwork hanging on the walls was by artists other than M. Martin; we imagined that they had been exchanged for his work, as some artists do this. M. Martin was unapologetic about the disorder and nonchalant style of the furnishings, and he swept through them as if, in fact, they were tidy and well-appointed.

Upstairs, he showed us three bedrooms furnished in the same random style, his studio, and a large, comfortable bathroom.

"You may occupy all of the rooms but not, of course, the studio," he explained. "Perhaps I shall not paint again. But I will save my work."

"Oh, we wouldn't need the studio," explained my wife. "There is more than enough space."

I could tell from her voice that she had decided we could live here, and, knowing her, I could also tell that she was already imagining herself sitting on the terrace on a sunny morning, drinking coffee or tea in the late afternoon, or cooking with the junkyard of utensils on that clumsy, old stove.

"The price you quoted on the telephone is agreeable to us," I said, "but what about heat? Doesn't it get cold in winter?"

M. Martin suddenly plunged back downstairs into the living room, and we followed. We found him standing next to a large oil stove at one end of the room.

"This will warm you," he exclaimed, thumping the hollow sides with his knuckles. "The oil man comes when you call him. Just ask for the small truck… It can pass through the gateway."

"And is there a school?" asked my wife, who placed her hand protectively on Jeremy's shoulders.

"Yes, down the driveway and just across the road is an *école primaire*. I know the *maître*, and he will accommodate your son."

"May I speak to my wife privately?" I asked. "Then we can tell you for sure."

"Certainly," he said. "But there is one last requirement. You must hire Annette. She will come once a week to clean. And, in the spring, you should allow her to have the cherries."

I must have looked puzzled, as M. Martin pulled me to the back window. Through it I could see three immense trees, barely able to hold their few last golden leaves, most of which had fallen into a thick, soft blanket around the trunks. Beyond it stood a small, cream-colored cement house with a red tile roof

THE CHERRY TREES

"Every year I let Annette pick the cherries. But beware. People stop on the road and climb over the wall to gather them. She is too old to prevent it. So you must be vigilant." He gave a French pronunciation to the last word for emphasis.

"That won't be a problem," I told him as I pulled Emily aside.

"We have to take it," I whispered. "The price is perfect, and the view is amazing, and the space..."

"It's a wreck," she said soberly, "but I know we can work it out. Tell him."

I did, and after a flurry of check-signing, further instructions, and hand-over of keys and another formal handshake, we climbed into the car and drove slowly down the tortuous road back to our hotel.

Everything was as M. Martin promised when we moved in the next week. He had arranged for Jeremy to attend the one-room country school at the end of our long driveway. Every morning, the schoolmaster gravely welcomed each child to school and shook the hands of every parent who accompanied a son or daughter. I always walked with Jeremy, who clutched his notebooks and pencils with a determination and energy that I had never noticed in him before. I nearly always took the occasion to speak with the schoolmaster. The *maître* was a jovial man with adults but treated his students with an ironic sternness. I was proud that my college French served me so well and used the occasion, frankly, to practice. I even began to comprehend the thick Niçoise accent of some of the other parents who delivered their children to the school.

"It is a strange part of France you have come to live in," the *maître* said fondly. "Before, there were nothing but peasants here and a few villas. You can still see a few greenhouses on the hill. Your own house belonged to a carnation farmer before M. Martin. I imagine you can still see an occasional straggler from the past—an orphan flower." It was clear he thoroughly enjoyed that turn of phrase. "But then, lately, a number of new houses have appeared, with swimming pools, gardens, and bourgeois children to be educated. What am I to do with such a mix? I have mostly peasant children who will never find a place here and a few sons and daughters of their rich and elegant new neighbors who will move to Paris to the *grandes écoles* as soon as they can."

"And now," I said, "a foreigner who is just learning to speak French."

"Well, Jeremy is the least of my problems. Trying to pour culture into the ears of these local children is a burden. Already so much in their lives has been

28

decided and foreclosed. Perhaps one will go to the university and find a position as a functionary of the state. But the rest will remain, clinging to a past they can only dream of, hoping to find everything they need to live in this quarter of the city, lacking imagination and possibility."

I thought it was a harsh judgment but perhaps fair. No doubt, the only real possession of value here was land—a view of the sea for sale as the waves of buildings from the city surged up the hill. It would not surprise me if the area would be completely transformed someday, and with it the school, the schoolmaster, and the neighborhood children might be swept away in a tide of affluence. That, I speculated, was his real worry: that his efforts to bring enlightenment to a few students who had hopes to continue in traditional ways would be swallowed up by real estate speculation. It was not his desire or his pleasure, given his slight Niçoise accent and unfashionable clothes, to educate the children of these rich newcomers who found him interesting and exotic but expendable.

M. Martin was also true to his word in the arrangement with Annette. On the first Thursday after we had installed our clothes and few possessions in the house, she arrived at nine. It was, in fact, the first time anyone had knocked at the front door. The noise of it echoed around the cement walls and across the bare, tile floors. I clattered down the staircase and opened the heavy oak door. There stood a small, energetic-looking woman. She was dressed in a plain, sleeveless, short, black dress. It was a sensible uniform that gave her thick arms and legs maximum room. In her left hand, she carried a blue, plastic bucket filled with bottles of cleaning fluid and rags. She wiped her feet on the mat, careful to make sure that I noticed this gesture, and spoke.

"For next week, you will need to buy cleaning supplies. Today, I have brought my own. I will give you a list."

"You must be Annette," I said, trying to give our conversation a more formal beginning. "Please come in. M. Martin told us all about you. We're delighted that you will work for us. And, yes, of course, I'll buy whatever you need for next week. We will be going into town on Saturday, and I'll take your list. Perhaps you can suggest the best store to buy supplies."

Annette entered and waited politely for me to lead her up a staircase that she had undoubtedly climbed a hundred times before. She had an air of reticence, as if she had never been in the house before and required guidance and instruction. I thought she was simply establishing our relationship, allowing me to take charge of something she knew far better than I. Just then, Jeremy came charging into the hallway between the kitchen and the dining room.

"Jeremy," I said, stopping him, "this is Annette. Remember M. Martin told us she would be working for us."

"Yes, Dad, I know…Hello," he blurted out in English. "Can I go out now?" And he turned and rushed down the staircase, probably to play with the stray black cat that had appeared when we drove up with our belongings.

"You'll have to forgive him," I said, switching back into French. "He hasn't learned how to meet people yet, and his French is just beginning. I hope, however, that you'll come to watch him on occasion, if we go to town to a movie or dinner."

"Surely, monsieur," she responded. "Do you have a television?"

"We are renting one beginning next week," I replied.

"That's fine then. I don't like to miss the dancing and music on Saturday night."

With this short conversation, Annette entered our lives and became, I supposed, a part of the family. Every Thursday morning, I watched her trudge up the hill along a path that led through the ruined carnation fields to the house. Her house was a small cottage that looked as if it were related to our own much larger building. Like our house, it was constructed of cement and had a roof made of the same thick, rounded tiles placed end overlapping end. Its walls had once been finished in an ocher plaster wash, but that had begun to fade and chip. Still, the brick red of the roof made it look charming from a distance, perfect to the blurred, hurried vision of a tourist, and similar to thousands of other country houses in the hills behind the Côte d'Azur.

The first time we left Jeremy and Annette together for an evening, I had a few misgivings. Jeremy was just learning French. Submerged in a completely foreign environment, he had almost stopped speaking, except when necessary or to complain bitterly that he hated French television because he couldn't understand what the cartoon characters were saying. Bugs Bunny in French! I spoke with the schoolmaster almost every day, and each time he assured me that Jeremy was making progress. "His brain is reorienting itself," he explained. "Soon enough he will be speaking perfectly: perfect accent and perfect word choice. It's as if we are pouring skills in his head until the day they will begin to spill over. Then you'll see."

In fact, I heard Jeremy say things to the other children—just parts of sentences, which was acceptable and natural enough to them anyway, but never anything whole, as if he could only just squeeze out hints at what was welling up beneath the surface. Clearly, the schoolmaster was right.

When Annette arrived punctually at seven that first night with a sonorous knock at the door, I told her not to worry if Jeremy was shy. He would probably play with some of his games—we had brought several—but he might like to watch television. I apologized for the black-and-white but added that it was a large screen. Annette remained quiet, and I assumed—in fact, I feared—that this meant disapproval.

"You can certainly watch what you want," I said. "And I'm sure you know how to work the set."

"Yes, monsieur," she replied. "Have a pleasant evening."

We climbed into our old, musty car and crunched slowly down the driveway to the road that led, in a series of switchbacks, ever closer to the glimmering city spread out below us.

It was about this time that Annette first mentioned the cherry trees at the edge of the garden that abutted the wall and the twisting road immediately beyond it that led into the *arrière-pays* behind Nice. The three large trees had heavy trunks and limbs that had been gnarled and knotted by slow growth and aggressive pruning. Like everything else around the house and the yard, they were scarred with the evidence of careful hands that had once forced the production of olives, carnations, and other fruit out of the stubborn, dry soil. Annette assured us that the grounds once contained a great many trees, including apricots and even peaches. But what remained were only three olive trees that bore reluctant, bitter green fruit and two loquat trees with their large, distinct leaves and soft, slightly rancid fruit that seemed to blemish at the touch. And, of course, there were the cherry trees. For some reason, it occurred to me that Annette thought of more than cherries when she saw them. Perhaps, I speculated, they were an emblem of her childhood, growing up in the beautiful, once-bountiful, and now-ruined space, of attending school, of marriage to a husband who had now disappeared. All that remained of those fertile days were the cherries, their perennial bounty, and the impassive wait for the approaching city to engulf the past.

THE CHERRY TREES

"But attention!" Annette cautioned me. "You can see the trees from the road, and it is easy to climb over the wall. When they are ripe, it is not just the birds who become thieves."

I wondered if it was the neighbors she suspected or passing tourists or children running home from school, hungry from their lessons. It was even possible for almost anyone to reach up from outside the wall and pull down one of the thick branches.

"Of course, you can have as many as you want, Annette," I assured her. "Consider them all yours. But tell me, what can you use them for? Sweet cherries won't last very long."

"Ah, monsieur," she replied with a sudden smile. "I make cherry compote. It lasts almost all year, perhaps until blossom time at Easter."

In that moment I was sure I understood the significance of the trees and the yearly ritual of picking and preparing. It was almost like an old, musty textbook on French peasant life had suddenly sprung to life. Here was an ancient custom, probably the only one that remained, that tied Annette to the land and her past. It was an utterly charming picture, as if someone had suddenly swept the dust from an open book to reveal a splendid colored illustration of peasants climbing ladders and filling oak buckets with bright red fruit. It could have been a portrait of our own property. This was why we had come to France! Now I understood.

I stopped this train of thought long enough to assure Annette. "You can be absolutely certain that I will allow no one to touch the cherries—not even the birds. Jeremy is a good lookout. And you know that we are here most of the time. I will inform anyone who tries to pick them that they belong to you."

Annette folded her arms across her chest and looked carefully into my eyes. I had the sense that a bargain had been proposed and accepted. Satisfied, she shuffled back toward her cottage through the dead grass and flowers.

Many times during that winter when Annette came to clean, we chatted about the neighborhood, the schoolmaster, M. Martin, who wrote occasionally from Paris, and the cherry trees. In the rain, which came occasionally then in cold, windy bursts, the gaunt branches of the trees turned a glistening black as the moisture dripped slowly down the slippery bark. Against the somber, black-blue sky, the trees, lit from the horizon, where the sun hung up in the clouds, presented an exaggerated picture of ruined order. The author of their shape—long gone for I could not imagine M. Martin on a ladder with pruning shears—had left his distinct mark, and the trees had the unnatural balance and candelabra shape that comes from years of effort. To me they represented the formality of the French countryside, where everything seemed to bear the mark of a human hand, where nature had been coaxed, even forced, into an extraordinary formal beauty.

By springtime, our neighborhood became, suddenly, a shock of green, punctuated by occasional flowers and blooming grasses growing helter-skelter. With no one to tend the garden, the disorder grew lusher and entangled around us, and I could see, even more than in the fall, that the land had been truly abandoned. For a while I fretted about this exuberant chaos, until, in exasperation, I drove down to a large nursery at the edge of Nice near the Var River to buy some plants. I chose several: petunias, dahlias, daisies, and even some sunflowers. When I returned, I pulled some old, shattered tools thick with cobwebs out of an immense closet on the ground floor and set to work clearing a small garden plot directly across from the terrace. The digging was difficult because the ground was heavy clay studded with white limestone pebbles almost as large as the pebbles that covered the local beaches. As I hacked at the clods, I imagined the difficult lives of peasants a hundred years ago, raising tender crops out of this harsh, sharp earth. When I finally finished, I had managed a fine-looking, round space of almost fifteen feet in diameter. I pushed the flowers into the ground, sowed the sunflowers, and carefully watered everything.

The real glory of the spring, however, was the cherry blossoms. In the still, early afternoons, they were alive with bees summoned from miles around in a ritual that I imagined must have been scores of years old. How they remembered was a puzzle, but this swarming and teeming busyness gave me a brief glimpse of the fertile energy that the season had once unleashed here on the hilltop. On occasion the sweet, dusty smell of blossoms drifted down to the house and spread a cloud of ruined petals over the terrace, making it difficult, if not impossible, at such moments, not to walk up under the trees to drink in an even more intense draft of their sweet perfume.

My garden, however, suffered almost as much as the cherry trees flourished, as if through some secret underground passageway the roots of the old trees sucked up the life of the new plants I had placed in the ground. Despite repeated watering, the delicate petunias began to shrivel, and the intense color of their flowers faded, leaving bare stalks to turn brown. Almost immediately, the same condition struck the dahlias and daisies, and soon the plot was reduced to a brown stubble of dying plants. I suspected that the ground was too alkaline, so I returned to the nursery and bought fertilizer and a new set of plants. I carefully mixed the soil and put in the new flowers.

For the first week or so, they also flourished, and I was sure that more days of sun and generous watering would produce a carpet of clashing purples, reds, and yellows. But suddenly, the same brown decay began to creep up the stems, and the flowers first bowed deeply, nodding to their imminent death, and then fell noiselessly to the ground. Within three or four days, the entire plot was reduced to stalks that looked like a miniature forest swept by fire.

That Thursday, when Annette appeared, I was anxious to ask her advice.

"You've seen my garden. What happened?" I asked.

Her face broke into a sad, distant smile.

"Well, of course, it was the snails. They come at night and eat around the stems of the plants. Perhaps you have seen their trails in the morning."

She must have been right because I suddenly recalled seeing the dew sparkling in slimy traces across the garden.

"But why didn't you tell me, Annette? Didn't you know it would happen?" I blurted out.

"Yes, I knew, but it wasn't my place to tell you, monsieur."

I experienced, at that moment, an intense feeling of estrangement, of being out of place, of my inability to push living roots into the hard French earth and alien clay of this place. I had fancied myself part of the neighborhood, learning its rituals and entering into its small conversations, but it all suddenly seemed unconnected and foreign.

"Well, there are the cherry trees," I replied. "I have nothing to do but watch them."

"Yes," she said. "I am counting on you."

As the weeks passed, the days became longer and drier, and the sky turned a relentless, metallic blue. In the distance, the Mediterranean lightened to a bright aquamarine, marking a sharp line across the horizon. In the yard, the tall spring grasses began to dry, and the stray flowers froze into splashes of dark yellow and gold. But the cherries gradually swelled as the deep roots of the trees sucked up moisture from far beneath the topsoil. As they turned red, they once again swarmed with insects, drawn by the anticipation of sweet, sticky pleasures. On occasion, a car would slow and then stop on the road. Its occupants would pretend to admire the trees until I appeared. No one climbed the wall,

34

but I was anxious for the moment Annette would decide to pick them, when the sweet, firm fruit hung exactly between perfection and decline.

Then one Saturday afternoon, we had just finished lunch, and Jeremy had run off into the garden to play, celebrating his release from school that morning. We were sipping the last drops of sweet black coffee on the terrace when suddenly he ran around the corner of the house.

"Papa, Papa," he cried (in French now because he had forgotten how to speak English). "There's someone in the garden picking cherries. He has a ladder and even a bucket!"

I put my cup down abruptly. The small spoon fell off the saucer and clattered onto the tile floor. I rushed downstairs and out along the path to the cherry trees. Jeremy was right. A man I had never seen before had set up a ladder and was filling a wooden bucket with cherries. I began to shout at him even before I reached the trees.

"Come down from there immediately," I cried. "You have no right to pick those cherries. They belong to the property here. Only the woman who lives in the cottage next door can have them!"

The man said nothing at first but then climbed slowly down from his perch. He took the basket in one hand, hoisted the ladder under his other arm, and slowly walked away from the trees.

"I am very sorry, monsieur," he said, looking back at me curiously.

I watched him leave the garden, and then I turned and went back to the house, proud of myself that I had saved the fruit for Annette.

On Thursday, when Annette returned, I greeted her anxiously. The cherries were more than ripe, and the birds had begun to flock around the trees, knocking off as much fruit as they ate, leaving it to rot bruised and brown on the ground. In another day or two, it would be too late.

"Annette," I asked, "why haven't you begun to pick the cherries? Jeremy and I will help you, if you'd like."

"Well, monsieur," she said sadly, "I have decided not to have the cherries this year."

"But why?" I exclaimed in amazement. "We've both been counting the days. You and I. And I've been vigilant. No one has succeeded in stealing them. But now the birds and the sun will finish them off!"

"No," she said firmly. "Not this year." Somehow I knew I should not ask again.

THE CHERRY TREES

The next morning when I walked Jeremy to school, I was determined to ask the Schoolmaster if he understood what could have changed Annette so abruptly. As we chatted in the courtyard in front of the school building, I related the strange conversation I'd had Thursday morning. He stopped me suddenly with a brusque gesture of his hand.

"Oh, yes. I know all about it," he laughed. "Everyone in the quarter has heard. You see, that was Annette's son you evicted from the ladder. He lives in the city, and every June he comes out to pick the cherries for his mother. Her preserves are famous in the area."

"But why didn't he say anything?" I exploded. "Why didn't she tell me? It was only a stupid misunderstanding on my part. She has to know I was doing it for her."

I walked slowly back to the house, and when I arrived, I changed into a long-sleeved shirt and old pants and shoes. I found a small stepladder under the house and carried it, with several plastic pails, down to the cherry trees. It was not easy work finding perfect fruit, because its prime had passed, and the sun was very hot. I worked the whole afternoon until sweat and sweet juice stung my eyes, and my fingers and hands turned to a dark brown with stains of a liquid that seemed immediately to impregnate my skin. Nevertheless, I succeeded in filling all my containers.

After I returned the ladder to the house, I picked up the heavy pails and walked down to Annette's cottage. I had never been inside or even this close because she always came to us. The building was small and dark, shuttered against the brilliant sunlight of the late afternoon. What had looked neat and even quaint from a distance now revealed itself in disorderly detail. There was a small vegetable garden and a few flowers but nothing of the exquisite composition of plants, cement, stone, and tiles that we could see in the beautiful neighboring hilltop villas. Perhaps this house had once been filled with energy and life, but now it, too, was decaying, waiting for the inevitable city to arrive.

I placed the pails of oozing fruit onto the cement slab in front of the house and knocked. The door opened immediately, and Annette came out quickly and closed the door behind her, preventing even a glimpse of the interior.

"Annette," I exclaimed, opening both hands in a gesture of gift-giving, "I've picked the cherries; here they are. I'm really sorry about what happened. I didn't know it was your son. But I still don't understand. Why didn't you tell me? Why didn't he say something?"

She looked at me distantly, almost as if I were a complete stranger, and said very slowly, "It wasn't my place to say anything, to be sure, monsieur. You could never understand that."

EINE KLEINE NACHTMUSIK

A blurry dusk began to fall over the Charles Bridge as the last portrait and etching vendors hurried to pack their wares into large canvas hampers. The solitary violinist urged his piece to an abrupt and dramatic finale, hoping for a few last coins to reward his flourish. But no one, apparently, noticed his battered case open on the ground or heeded his musical plea. Tourists were still thick, getting a last glimpse of the sun setting over the west bank of the city. A Japanese man had stopped to take one final photograph of a couple leaning against one of the statues atop the supporting pillars of the bridge. The softening backdrop of the evening made its flash brittle and annoying. Carefully and deliberately, she began, conscious of the verbal compromise they had both made and nervous that she might break it, "Czechoslovakia certainly is grand, even if it is overrun with Italians. What could they possibly be doing here in such numbers? What are we near? Milano, maybe? Torino? I can imagine the buses lumbering over the Alps or just plowing through Austria. I never know why people travel in such large groups. It has to be all about waiting."

This was safe enough to say: to question the travel motives of others, to wonder out loud why someone chose this tourist spot over the next. It had been their argument, running now for three years, although it was also clear that he had won, that they would always—if *always* was to be the future—do it his way. Patricia stiffened slightly, shifted her cheap black travel purse over her shoulder, and glanced sharply at Larry. "A perfectly ordinary person," she said to herself with admiration, "that no one would ever suspect of such strangeness." And, in fact, he was almost ordinary, athletic, but now stooped as he bent forward to balance the unnatural weight of his backpack. His dark hair and mustache might have given him an exotic, even attractively sinister look but for a fullness around the mouth that negated any such impression. And his exaggerated cheeks, slightly bronzed by the day's sun, erased all possibility of mystery.

"What about that concert?" she continued, bringing up something that demanded a real and immediate decision. "If we want to go, we have to decide about dinner. Now or later. It would probably take a couple of hours. So maybe a snack now and a stroll or a fast bite somewhere and then off to the church." "Was she pushing it too much, this suggestion of a plan?" she wondered. There were limits, of course, but she wanted him to decide. It was a great comfort to her not to make decisions.

"Either way," he said. "That is, if you really want to go. I'm puzzled by the program. Everything in every venue is the same, the same bill of fare: churches, concert halls, everywhere. Do you think that this country has a ministry of tourist music left over from the old Warsaw Pact days? So there can't be any competition, just mechanical repetition. I wonder if the program ever changes? Maybe it's *Eine kleine Nachtmusik* every night all over the city. Sure, there may be some pieces—Smetana's *My Country* instead of Pachelbel's *Canon*—but it's still the top-ten classical music hits of all time. That's what tourists can do to a place. They reduce a great musical tradition to MacMusik. You shouldn't encourage them."

Patricia looked at him and laughed. "You're just saying that because you think it's funny. Although I know you're right. But it's not the music but the atmosphere I want. To sit in one of those lovely Baroque churches with the lights reflecting on the gilt and those wonderful, slurry acoustics. I love to hear music—any music—bouncing around the stone pillars and statues, coming up at you off the floor and from all around, making echoes within echoes." She was almost breathless with excitement and wonder at her own enthusiasm for something so clichéd.

"Well, I think we need to go if you feel that way. Where does that come from? You're not the same at home. So enthusiastic here!"

"It's the city…I just love…"

"Don't," he said firmly. "Don't say it…"

"So we can go, even if it is a cliché," she said, quickly backing off from talking about Prague.

"I suppose so," he said. "If you want to. We just need to choose one of the concerts; it doesn't matter which. You decide because any one will do." He abruptly began to walk on, picking his way skillfully through the now-diminishing crowd. She followed.

"Strange," she thought. "You learn things about people you never suspected before, and somehow, even if they are surprising and odd, it doesn't matter. You accommodate. Of course, there is the quirky way he chooses a place to visit, but more, too." Now, as she watched him plunge ahead, she realized a certain curiosity about the way they walked—or didn't walk—together. He liked to stay one or two paces ahead of her. Every time she caught up and touched his arm even slightly, he slowed, as if she had given him a tug on a leash. But just as surely, he gradually went faster until she had to catch him again.

"You really have to slow down for me," she often said. And she firmly believed that he thought they were walking together. But why? she asked herself. Why did he want to walk in front of her? It couldn't be the pace, because whenever she hurried, he sped up slightly. She called it his "foraging," his need to be out front, scouting and leading. Maybe this was natural, coming from something so inborn or ingrained that it had no history, no beginning, and certainly no way of being changed. Curiously, she admired this, as if it revealed an instinct for command.

She watched his hips swing into a faster gait as he reached the end of the bridge and the central avenue of the city. Of course, there were no cars—they were banned, and (she was even more grateful) there were no bicycles; there were just human obstacles, people walking unsteadily, turning abruptly around to comment to a friend or stopping to look into a store window or savor a view that was recognizable from a postcard. She was like that herself, wanting to pause on a whim, to look at every shop display. This was her almost-unconscious way of shopping or doing the preliminaries, looking for the most popular and common tourist versions of traditional handicraft to identify what might, under all the glitter or plastic, be indigenous pottery shapes and styles or wooden craft. Here in Prague it seemed to consist, surprisingly, of Russian nested dolls, so brightly painted and compactly displayed that from a distance they looked like a gilt mosaic. Or painted eggs. Or wooden toys shaped into chess sets and puppets and dolls with gnarled and pinched carved faces. Not that any of it would really do for a child. There was something too cruel—or not cruel but wizened and sinister—about these dolls and Pinocchios. They seemed to embody the spirit of a medieval trickster, someone who would pinch a child if you turned out the lights.

Thinking all this, she fell behind, now only catching a glimpse of Larry's swinging backpack. She knew that he was, nonetheless, paying attention to her hesitant gait, and that he wouldn't really lose her. It was a game they played or, rather, two roles they took on: his consisting of the determined pursuit of a goal, a place, geography, as if tourism accomplished something on a list of to-do's, and hers consisting of more abstract and distracted meandering toward the unexpected and the accidental.

It was, she thought, a summing-up of their relationship: his absolute certainty, the decisiveness of his mind, his ability to turn everything into a coherent system. This only made her less-orderly, haphazard way of living seem like a virtue to her and a challenge for him. And they both enjoyed the banter, the testiness, the flirtation with anger and frustration that frequently marked their talk. There was something almost erotic in this game of differences, an extreme and exaggerated and completely unrealistic and playful sense of gender roles that made their arguments almost like sexual encounters. Of course, there was the danger of going too far, particularly if she seriously questioned Larry's "scheme of life," as he had named it.

Realizing she had stopped in front of a darkened antique shop of no particular consequence, she shook off these thoughts, gazed carefully at her image faintly reflected in the dusty glass, and looked around for him. He was twenty yards in front, turned toward her with his arms folded like a breastplate in front of him, watching. She quickly hurried on.

"I'm terribly sorry," she explained, "but there is so much to see, and I want to take it all in."

"I can see that," he said and turned to continue down the street.

"Wait just a minute," she asked. "I want to know where we are going I've got the map here." She pulled out the glossy, green *Michelin Guide* and turned to the page with the plan of the city. Placing her finger on it, she traced their movements from the bridge, through the plaza, and onto what was clearly only a side street.

"I think we are heading the wrong way. We need to go back and then turn left."

He looked at the map and flicked her finger away from the spot, placing his own forefinger on the map. She felt a sudden flash of rage. "No, you mustn't say anything," she told herself. "It's not worth it to protest."

"In fact," he said and demonstrated with a nod of his head, "we are going exactly in the right direction if you want to get to the concert at St. Thomas

Church. I've figured out a shortcut. So let's be going." He resumed a brisk pace, not waiting for her.

"Please," she said, "just a minute. I want to see things. You can't be noticing anything at this pace. How will you ever enjoy the city if you don't slow down?"

"If I slow down, I'll never finish. You know that. And, by the way, we are seeing a country, not a city. Otherwise, it ruins everything, puts things completely out of order. Remember, C as in *the Czech Republic*, not P for *Prague*. Spending time only in one city is our compromise."

"Yes, I know, Larry, but I can't believe you actually saw those lovely stores back there—the beautiful porcelain, the puppets and wooden toys."

"Oh, I saw them all right, including the antique stores." And he began to move again.

So they trudged on, Larry confidently and she with growing doubts. The direction seemed wrong, and she was tired and hungry and worried. It couldn't be in the direction they moved because the pedestrian street had opened out into traffic and there was a tramway line just ahead of them. She could see an articulated red coach just pulling up to a crowded stop in the gloom.

"It's not right, Larry. I know the church is in the other direction. Back, closer to the bridge, but north I think. I don't want to be late, but hurrying in the wrong direction doesn't help."

He looked at her sharply and, chastening her with a glance, but turned and led her according to the direction she suggested. It was getting late, and they had only about twenty minutes to reach the church, buy tickets, and find a place. The sun still emitted a fuzzy glow to their left, but it was no longer bright enough to create more than blurred, soft shadows. Lights began to pop on in the little shops, and the streetlamps came on all at once—like lighting in a dark theater. The city was exactly that, she thought: a play whose acts were day, dusk, and night.

"Don't you think Prague is just like a stage, where every vantage point is designed for the spectator's point of view?"

He stopped suddenly, took one shoulder in his firm left grip, and slowly said, "Look, Patricia. You promised not to say that name. I know you think I'm silly, that my life's project is just some sort of control fantasy, that I'm a borderline something or other. But I just won't see things out of order or even discuss them that way. C is for *Czech Republic*, and P doesn't come up for years.

43

That's the way I intend to keep it. The whole world is comprehensible that way. Otherwise, traveling is just giving into impulse, like your window-shopping. Or going to the nearest cheap place, like your Italians. And anyway, you agreed to the terms."

"Yes, I did," she said. "I agreed. And I suppose I understand, although I still don't really know why one would pick Austria, like we did, over Algeria or Armenia or Argentina or even Alabama or Azerbaijan? You could end up exhausting one letter with a lifetime."

"It's the sense of order that matters," he responded. "I'm not trying to visit every country in the world. Who would want that? But this is how I place limits on things. Leave it at that and promise to let me have my illusions; you certainly have yours."

She nodded because he was right. She had said almost the same thing last time they talked about it. She would make the same objections the next time, but she would always give in. Anyway, he didn't criticize her wandering, her directionless course, or the concerts she dragged him to. It amused him.

They walked another hundred yards and into a square that held the church they sought. Two young men, incongruous in jeans under long red robes, emerged from the church, each carrying a long brass trumpet. They stopped before a music stand set out in the square, blared a perfunctory fanfare, and then suddenly retreated back inside. Larry approached the ticket table that had been set with CDs and brochures about other city performances. He bought two tickets and picked up one of the CDs to inspect.

"Look," he said, "you can get *Eine kleine Nachtmusik* played by three different groups. In fact, look at this." He held up a brochure. "They're each one playing it tomorrow night, too."

She looked hard at him before she spoke. "It's all right. I know it's a cliché. But let me have that. I like clichés. I like tourist trinkets. I like phony folk art, and I like familiar music. Let me have my illusion of being back in the Baroque world. Let me have my fantasy. Back then I would have been sitting in just this church listening to this music on such a night."

"You know it's an illusion," he said, smiling, "and I love you for that."

"Oh, yes, of course it is," she replied. And they moved quickly into the brightly lit nave of the church in search of a seat. There were only a few other patrons inside, so the scuff of their shoes on the stone paving echoed around the walls and came back to them. To her, the music had already begun.

THE DIVORCE

He hated them all, or at least he thought he did sometimes. Not his cousins, of course, with their broad, singsong accents, but all the older people. There were so many that he could never remember their names, or maybe he forgot them purposely. Aunts and uncles and great-aunts and great-uncles and cousins once removed, a huge family tree heavily laden with cadaverous elderly relatives that he denied could really be his own. He belonged, by choice, to no branch of that heritage. He was a child of the north; his parents had escaped this hot, humid place of their birth, and he was not of it. But the reunion had happened every summer since he could remember. He dreaded it for a hundred reasons he could not even articulate. Why they had to go was a mystery, except that his mother, as the time approached, grew more animated, quicker in her step, more apt to smile for no reason.

Last year and this year and the next would be the same. After a long train ride, he and his mother would descend onto the grimy platform at Prairieville where the sun caught flecks in the concrete and made them flicker like fake diamonds. The station itself was a low brick building with a green tile roof, around which hung an atmosphere of ozone, diesel fumes, and coal cinders, all poached by the brilliant, hot light into a miasma of smells. He liked this moment; there was something intriguing about railroads, perfect for imagining himself traveling along, to be always in motion toward some strange place, and toward growing up. Then he would be able to say no, finally, to coming here. He wished that his father would travel with them, just once, but he always took the airplane for a long weekend, not the six or seven days his mother spent here and he invariably took a long taxi ride from St. Louis that cost a great deal. He knew this because his mother always admonished, "Why, it's almost as expensive as taking the train all the way from Chicago." His mother, if she could not control what his father spent, could at least watch carefully over her own expenses, and she would never fail to make a pointed, if oblique, comment about his father's extravagances.

THE DIVORCE

His parents never argued about money; in fact, they never argued about anything in front of him. But sometimes, at night, in bed, he overheard a sudden tone that broke into his sleep, a word said in anger maybe or a muffled sob. He wasn't sure, but it always woke him up instantly. He would listen, then, intently, as if he could wring more sounds out of the air by concentrating his attention, hoping to understand what it meant, what was the matter. But his efforts never amounted to anything, and he would suddenly find himself with frozen, clenched fists and rigid arms and legs. Only gradually on such nights would he be able to fall back to sleep.

His aunt Flo, a big, blowsy, talkative woman, always met them at the train. She usually arrived ten or fifteen minutes late, during which time his mother sat rigid on the waiting bench, suitcases neatly arranged at her feet. She sat the whole time, becoming straighter and straighter, one ankle crossed over the other, with arms folded across her chest. He knew she was furious, although she would never admit it.

"That train is just never on time," his aunt would always say, as if to explain, bursting into the waiting room and sweeping over to hug them. "Now come along. I've left the motor running in the car. Everyone is back home." She would then lead them happily to the rumbling station wagon, chattering as she opened doors and put the luggage into the back.

Aunt Flo was his father's sister and was just tolerated by his mother, who responded to her constant stream of conversation with an articulate silence. His mother always withdrew when confronted with a situation she disapproved of, becoming more ladylike and prim and exuding a cold atmosphere of censure that could freeze the most animated conversation. This was especially effective with children. He knew this because his friends walked gingerly around his house when they came to play, declining to stir up the raucous messes that they made in their own homes. It was sometimes as if he lived in a museum whose treasures were common emotions carefully labeled, framed, and displayed as if rare and inaccessible. Aunt Flo, of course, never reacted to these controlling silences, and sometimes he wondered if his mother did not secretly admire her persistence and nonchalance. He always responded to this warm bath of talk and confusion, and thought, impatiently, about the swimming, hiking, and games he would play with his cousins. At such moments he even wondered why he so dreaded these southern vacations.

But, of course, he knew. The reunion brought two large families together, two clans that had a long history of enmity between them reaching back to the Civil War. He understood this because several of his uncles had drawn him aside to tell stories and show him photographs of tall, stiff, shaggy men in uniforms, standing in the midst of a lounging troop or their hands resting on rifles. On his father's side, the family was mostly Confederate, having moved up recently from Kentucky into Southern Illinois, bringing with them their hunting dogs, shabby furniture, and broad, Southern speech. Their destination had been his mother's town, built from a land grant to her family. They were merchants, railroad telegraph officials, and schoolteachers, and the old photographs he saw of this side featured men in dark business suits standing in front of delivery wagons hailing his mother's last name or in family pictures in front of houses he still recognized near Main Street. But the two clans had fought on different sides in the war, and despite a common understanding between them (a truce brought on by proximity, common interest, and even marriage), certain hotheads had made the war personal and deadly.

"That's your great-great-uncle Edward. He was a Confederate doctor. Served in the army all along the Mississippi and just south of here. The tales he told of operating during battle…And you know what that means, don't you, Tommy?"

He didn't know but never quite dared to ask.

"Your great-great-grandfather, he explained once, "was the first grocer here in Prairieville. When the war came, he enlisted, not like some families around here who saved their boys by buying Irish substitutes. You know, they were just opening the mines in those days, and there were lots of hands and arms to go around if you didn't want to serve. But your great-grandfather knew his duty. He wouldn't talk about it much, but he saw things you would never want to see again."

"But what would people think if you didn't go into the army?" he asked.

"That you had a lot of money and not much in the way of courage," was the reply.

"What did Great-Grandfather see?" he asked.

"I'll tell you when you grow up," his uncle chuckled. "Just remember for now that once upon a time your mother's family and your father's family looked at each other from opposite ends of a rifle."

THE DIVORCE

He could hardly imagine these old uncles fighting a war, and he wondered why they talked about it so gravely and yet also laughingly. He hoped that when he grew up such unpleasant family memories would not haunt him. Even if he did once wake up to a nightmare in which his uncles were chasing him along a railroad track shouting, "Boy, you have to fight; you can't escape!" he would never visit this place when he grew up. He was sure.

Besides his aunt, there was his grandmother on his father's side, a fastidious, ancient person who invariably dressed in shades of apricot or rose, as if she considered herself a delicate fruit or flower. She had long, silky black hair that was highlighted with silver; she brushed it with long, tired strokes in front of the mirror on her dressing table at night. Every night she would then make a long braid and, before going to bed, don her flowered nightshirt and make the rounds of the doors and windows, closing each firmly to seal up the house even in the cloying summer heat, leaving only one upstairs window open. His mother often complained to him and to his father about this habit. His father once said to him jokingly, "She can't sleep unless the house is closed and shrouded. It's not so bad for a few days."

"A few days for you...a week for me," his mother had reminded him.

His grandmother served a menu when they visited that never failed to fascinate and repel him. She refused to eat anything uncooked, and so even the fruit they rarely consumed was stewed in heavy syrup to the point of disintegration. Looking at her he sometimes wondered if eating this boiled composition eventually made one's face pucker, as if the soft, mushy texture was infectious. Her lips and her eyes were furrowed with deep, soft lines that, despite the considerable powder and rouge she applied, made her look gaunt. When she hugged him, once carefully when they arrived and once again when they departed, he could smell the powder she left on his skin, and the soft brush of her cheek felt like a piece of moist velvet.

For him, being only ten years old, there was no clear place in this extended family. The "menfolk," as he heard them referred to as, scattered early in the morning on a series of never-ending errands or golf matches that invariably ended up at the local Elks Club. He could not imagine the attraction of such a place; he had seen it once from the street, pointed out by his mother with in a gesture of disapproval. When his father and his uncle returned in the evenings, they would sometimes ask what he had done during the day, although he never gave them another sentence of explanation beyond "oh, not much." They would sit on the porch sipping bourbon and talking in the clipped and referential way that men do when they have spent considerable time together. Their conversation was nine-tenths submerged, and the subjects always eluded him. But it was pleasant to listen to the droning mixture of different accents punctuated by silence and then the sudden resumption of words or occasional laughter.

This would continue until a late dinner, prepared by the women who fought quietly over ingredients, cooking time, and what and where to serve it. Most of the time, his grandmother prevailed and overwhelmed them with fried chicken, mashed potatoes, and huge bowls of limp, overcooked vegetables. Only rarely did his mother triumph over his aunt and grandmother, and on those occasions he recognized a change of texture, a familiar scale of servings, a reticence and parsimony that contrasted with the usual extravagance of their Southern Illinois fare...

Whatever his day was like, with swimming trips or visiting, there were always long stretches of time when he and his cousins lay out under the huge hickory tree in the backyard, reading or talking or planning some adventure that never seemed to happen because it required preposterous distances and fantastic equipment. These long, empty spaces were filled with odd concentrated staring at long leaves of grass, ants, and other insects clambering intrepidly over the huge objects in their miniature world, of feeling dusty wind blowing pollen, and of smelling the sweet, lemony perfume of the nearby magnolia tree. He associated his time in Prairieville with these monotonous afternoons when nothing seemed to happen, when time moved along to the slow metronome of the rising and falling buzzing of the cicadas. So, when he told his father and uncle "nothing," he meant to report accurately on these languorous afternoons, although not on his thoughts that, at the same time, raced from subject to subject: his friends at home, his curiosity about and dislike for his uncles, and the nights at home when he thought he heard his mother sobbing.

"Children," his father said, "are meant to be seen and not heard," a sentiment which quickly brought nods of approbation from his uncles and his grandmother. The idea was intriguing to him, and there were times when he imagined he could hold his breath, become invisible, and float unseen into a room filled with adults, his body dissolved by an act of will, his mind reduced to seeing and recording their conversations. Then, at last, he thought, he might understand what they were saying, what they meant by the references he could not identify, and what they seemed to be hiding from him. Perhaps, even, he would understand his mother and father and why she sat so primly with a look of disapproval on her face and why he never seemed to look directly into her eyes.

But, of course, his father did not mean this about children; instead, he was simply waiting for some sign of maturity, for him to show the first signs of leaving his boyhood behind. Then his father would talk to him.

This was the reason that that summer he decided he wanted to attend the family-reunion cocktail party. He would prove himself mature enough to be with the adults—this one time—to discover the secrets of the words he had only half-overheard and -understood. He would discover why his mother so deeply and thoroughly enjoyed this one late evening of the trip and why she put aside her customary harsh look and became open and demonstrative.

"You're not old enough, Tommy," was the unsurprising response he received to his plea.

"But, Mom. I've always wanted to go, and I'm plenty old enough. I can wear my suit. You brought it, remember. And, anyway, you promised." He said all this, laying out as many reasons as possible and without interruption, hoping he might hit upon one that was convincing.

"The suit is for church," she replied. "And, of course, you can go eventually. Just not this year."

"I could empty ashtrays and help out. You always say that Aunt Flo needs help and won't hire anyone. I could do that."

By accident, he had stumbled upon a reason, and his mother smiled.

"Yes, perhaps," she said. "I'll have to ask your grandmother what she thinks. In the meantime, don't tell your father. I don't believe he would approve."

He was not exactly sure why this argument had worked, but he knew that his mother had often said, "Aunt Flo isn't much of a housekeeper. She ought to get somebody." His presence might be his mother's gesture of criticism.

The reunion party always began late in the afternoon of a Saturday so that both clans could arrive on time. His mother's family had dispersed into the small towns surrounding Prairieville to become their principal doctors, lawyers, and store owners. They came in two or three cars, which poured out aunts and uncles onto the front lawn, laughing and carrying dishes covered in thick, creamy linens. His mother always cried out with joy when she saw them and greeted them with a warmth and emotion that puzzled him and almost made him jealous.

As far as he could see, his father's family was exactly the same, for they, too, had dispersed into the nearby area to become important businessmen. His aunts had the same pale, fading red hair, and all of them carried some contribution to the meal that even the children would be invited to attend at eight. Only he had received permission to help out with the cocktail party. He would not have to leave with the rest of the children after they greeted each newcomer. And only he, among his cousins, wore much more than a clean change of clothes, and the suit he had pulled on made him feel stiff and hot but considerably more mature than his more casual relatives.

"My, aren't we the handsome young man, Tommy?" was invariably the remark of each new couple. "You've certainly grown some since last summer." He and his cousins bore the hugs and crushing handshakes of these intimate strangers. But this time he assured each one of them: "I'm helping Aunt Flo with the party. That's why I've got my suit on."

That evening, at first, he hung back in the crotch of the living room archway, almost afraid to enter the hot, lively room. But, catching a stern glance from his mother, who had carefully instructed him on his duties, he began to glide quietly around the room, almost invisibly, riding the waves of laughter, dodging the sudden movements and shifts of the older, taller adults who unconsciously made way for him. He picked up glass ashtrays filled with cigarettes, bits of lipstick-stained napkins, and toothpicks bearing the faint traces of black olives. He took these carefully into the kitchen, dumped them into the waste can, and wiped them out before replacing them on the tables around the room. He carefully watched the ice in the large china bowl on the drinks table and from time to time carried a small bucket out of the kitchen to refill it. During the first half hour or so, a few of his aunts and uncles, his parents, and most of the other guests who came regularly to the reunion remarked on his presence.

"Well, that's nice of you, Tommy." "What a big boy!" "I hope they're paying you well."

And then they stopped noticing him as he moved quietly around the room. It was very like what he had imagined it would be like to float unseen in the presence of their talk—and yet also not at all, for he could still not understand their conversation. The words, of course…he understood those, but

THE DIVORCE

what were they really saying? What accounted for the laughter that burst out unexpectedly? Why did they just talk and talk?

He thought this and watched even more closely. His grandmother fascinated him. She was wearing a rose-colored dress with a stiff collar that contrasted with her dark, streaked hair. She sat for most of the afternoon in a high-back chair, and he noticed that the room seemed to circulate around her, as everyone stopped to say something to her, to compliment her appearance, to exchange a memory.

His aunt Flo was a startling contrast to the formality of his mother. She wore a shiny, blue-green dress with a low neckline. He noticed her heavy jewelry because his mother had often remarked on it: a large gold chain ending in a red-gold, heart-shaped locket and a matching bracelet with the same motif. She sat heavily on the couch, one hand dangling a glass filled with bourbon and ice cubes, which she swirled dangerously when she wasn't sipping from it. The other hand held a cigarette. He could see the heavy red smear from her lips on the filter. She sat with one leg on the ground and the other slightly curled and wedged between her calf and the edge of the couch. There was something intriguing about her—and also her partner on the couch.

He recognized the man as someone he always called "Uncle Fred" but who, in fact, was merely a friend of the family. He was a large, excitable man with sweaty, furrowed skin and big, soft hands that swept carelessly across nearby objects as if out of control: over his knees, the coffee-table, the back of the couch, and, once or twice lightly, over Aunt Flo's bare arm and shoulder. Their conversation was deep and intense, and they appeared to be ignoring everyone else in the room.

Tommy looked around excitedly, searching for his uncle and "Uncle" Fred's wife. "Why did they do this?" he wondered. "Why didn't his aunt and uncle stay together at their own party? After all, they're married."

He looked for his mother and father but only saw his father standing in the corner chatting casually with a woman he did not recognize. He wondered where his mother had gone, and picking up his ice bucket, he walked quickly into the kitchen to find her. No one was there, so he filled the bucket and plunged back into the room. Nothing had changed. His Aunt Flo was now laughing broadly at something Fred had whispered to her. For some reason he began to feel sick: a wave of nausea started to rise in his stomach. His knees felt

52

weak, and his suit became washed in sweat. "Why don't they stop?" he thought to himself. "What's wrong with them? Where's Mom? Why isn't she there?"

He ran out of the room and upstairs to the bedroom. Without turning on the light, he sat down on his bed and began to sob, cupping his hands over his ears to blot out the muffled noises that reached him from the party.

Much later that night and in bed after the dinner party, during which he happily retreated to the children's table, his mother slowly opened his door and entered. She still wore her party dress, half-covered in the front by a damp apron that smelled of soap and dishes.

"What's the matter, Tommy? Why did you leave? Did you get tired? I wondered if it was a good idea for you to work so hard."

"Nothing happened. I'm fine," he said stiffly.

"Well, it must be something. I know you don't like to come here, but it's for your father and me. We don't get to see our families that often."

He felt guilty that she understood this much. "No," he blurted out, "that's not it. I'm fine!"

"Really, Tommy, you shouldn't be so judgmental. These are our friends and your own family."

"Leave me alone," he begged. "I'm fine." But he could feel the tears welling up in his eyes and a blush of shame blazing across his face. She put her hand on his shoulder and squeezed it slightly.

"What is it, Tommy?" she asked, putting her hand gently on his cheek.

"All right, I'll tell you!" he confessed, turning away abruptly. "It's Aunt Flo. They're going to get a divorce, aren't they? She wasn't with him at all tonight."

"What on earth do you mean? With whom?" she asked sharply.

"I mean that Aunt Flo shouldn't have been talking to that man—Uncle Fred—like that. It was almost like they were married. And he's not even her husband."

She looked at him for a long time without a word, but he could read the shifting emotions in her eyes as she sought an explanation. Then, suddenly, she laughed gently. It made him cringe with embarrassment.

"I think I understand. Yes, I know, Tommy. It's all right. You're worried, aren't you? You think your father and I are going to get a divorce! I can imagine what made you think that." She reached her arms around him and pulled him up to her, enveloping him in her wet apron.

THE DIVORCE

"But it's not true at all Tommy. No!" she cried, "I'm so sorry I let you go to the party. I was wrong. There's just too much still that you can't understand. You really are much too young."

THE GIFT

I looked up because my mother became abruptly silent for a moment before ending her conversation. "Yes, of course you are," she stated with finality and replaced the black receiver carefully in its cradle. I watched her stiffen her back and then begin to fidget with the handkerchief in her lap in a way I knew always signaled some sort of inner turmoil, as if the conflict had to work its way out through her hands before she could articulate it. She cleared her throat sharply and then, suddenly, laughed a single, clear note of amusement that she caught and stopped in midair. Looking up, she saw me across the living room reading a magazine. Of course, she knew I was there all the time, watching her, but in her self-absorption, she had closed off her awareness of anything in the room but her own concentration.

"It's really nothing," she said, answering my unspoken question. "Just that Cousin Vera is coming to town."

"But you don't seem very happy about it," I replied.

"No, not really. But it's fine. We'll make do."

From experience I knew the burden of those last three words and the futility of objecting to them. They meant the grudging acceptance of necessity, some stressful duty imposed upon us, sometimes by an unexpected and unwelcome momentary shortage as in not having enough chairs at the dining room table or enough beds to accommodate visitors or enough potatoes for a hungry guest. These were minor domestic versions of coping that required a small sacrifice, but there were also larger ones, usually having to do with the unreasonable demands of my mother's very large family. Cousin Vera was probably the most trying of our make-do obligations.

"I think we are stuck with her for a week," said my mother. "So, you'll have to sleep in your brother's room and clear away some of your things from your dresser."

"But why here? There have to be some other aunts and uncles who can put her up. She always stays here!"

THE GIFT

"Nothing to be done about it. You know—maybe I shouldn't tell you—but everyone leaves town when she announces a visit. Or they say they are leaving, or they are suddenly too busy or sick or just won't answer the telephone or the door. So we'll have to make-do. It's only a week."

My mother and Cousin Vera (her cousin once removed and thus twice as distant from me) were two versions of the same pattern and cut from the same family sampler, although they were a generation apart. In fact, all the Porter women looked alike, particularly after middle age had begun to erase the sharp distinctive lines of their features and to turn their brown or red or blond hair to a sparse, tarnished silver. All of them had the same faintly freckled skin that with age gradually lost its opaque luster, allowing blotches of muted red and brown to show through. Age, it seemed, became concentrated in their hands as knotted strands of blue veins laced across their knuckles from finger to wrist like the exposed roots of old trees. Yet they all possessed a sort of nervous beauty, unsure or even ashamed of itself, or repressed perhaps, and enhanced only vaguely by any makeup, as if artificial colors and creams and powders were only meant to be applied symbolically: signs hastily put on before greeting guests or going out in public but never used with any confidence that they were more than a social obligation. There was something puritanical about the studied, careless, and inexpert way of this manner of application.

Porter voices were rich and high, with a hint of musicality cultivated by years of singing in church choirs. As far as I knew, none of them had ever been a soloist or sought any formal training, but they all had spirited voices, and most of the women, at least, could play the piano competently. This minor musical bent must have appealed to their sense of order and propriety, providing a perfect lesson in the way life should be lived, with an ordered beauty, achieved by following prescribed inflections and set notations.

My mother was, as everyone said, a "handsome" woman. That always seemed odd to me when I heard it pronounced and especially now as I think back on the moment of Vera's visit. Why use such a distinctly masculine word to describe a woman? Not, of course, that there was anything even vaguely mannish about her, except that she was tall and large-boned, and beauty in a woman seems to require something diminutive or vulnerable about it. Handsome meant attractive in a way but at the same time slightly large or imposing or unapproachable.

Cousin Vera, on the other hand, was a tiny woman with all of the Porter features compressed and sharpened to fit her diminutive frame. She wore her hair—auburn even at the age of seventy—in a mound on the top of her head, now with a single layer of gray wound around it as if a symbol of years. My mother said that it was the most beautiful hair she had ever seen but that Vera began wrapping it up before she was twenty and had never changed her hairstyle after that. Such a configuration lent itself to hats, and she almost always wore a modest cloche with a hint of a lace veil when she arrived or went calling. She also wore suits, unlike the other women of her generation who had begun to dress in shapeless and faded pastels. Perhaps her clothing was her sign of difference, a visual reminder that she had left our small town in Southern Illinois to live and work in Washington, DC, as a government clerk. No one ever said what she did exactly, nor did she volunteer the information, but to her, at least, this employment was a badge of self-improvement and independence, far better than settling to be a schoolteacher, which is what my other aunts ended up doing. She often commented on their lack of imagination.

Vera's disapproving eyes were what one noticed first about her—even before the red hair and the prim green outfits. Lighting on something or someone, they triggered a slight frown and an almost inaudible "uh-huh"—an interior agreement that seemed to confirm her expectation of discovering some physical or moral shortcoming as soon as it entered her field of vision. When this criticism took the shape of words, and it did so frequently, it was sometimes indirect and always unexpected—rhetorical questions of disapproval. "Your children have terrible posture." "Don't you think that dress is too grown-up for a girl of her age?" "Is Cousin Bill still drinking?"

Because my Mother cleaned our house relentlessly, scrubbing even the newness out of every recent acquisition, Vera had no criticism to make of us in general, although I sometimes believed that she objected to boys on moral grounds.

Her formality and fastidious manner made it difficult for me to believe that she had once been married—to Ralph. No one said much about him, and he had died several years ago, unremarkably except for a brief squib undoubtedly written by Vera, herself for the local paper. Still, I could not imagine her, in a sea of red hair, loosened on a pillow, in the abandon of passion. The couple had been childless, although they took in her niece, Abigail, when her sister and her husband were killed in an automobile accident. I had never seen Abigail because she now lived in California and, apparently, never even went back to Washington to see Vera and certainly never came to Southern Illinois to see us.

Vera's visit that August when I was just preparing to leave home for the University of Chicago was like many others that I could recall from childhood. All the special edges and unique spaces of most of those memories have now disappeared or, rather, merged into one picture of an endless dinner. With all of us gathered at the dining room table, my father served each plate, seemingly oblivious to what was happening around him or perhaps secretly amused by my mother's attempt to deflect the extreme declarations of her cousin. As always, Vera held court. She began and ended each short burst of conversation with a pointed question about someone or something followed by a sharp, almost-unanswerable comment. There were times when I knew these exchanges were very amusing, and I was tempted to laugh, partly because I thought I detected a flash of irony in her eyes. But I was afraid to let on—reluctant to offend my mother who always tried to soften Vera's stern judgments with an apology or an explanation that often just provoked a bolder assertion. I admired this peace-making but also saw its futility because Vera wasn't really listening and had no intention of compromising her views.

However, that particular visit gave rise to a family story that improved (and worsened) with each telling. One heavy, muggy Sunday afternoon, sitting in the living room after dinner, Vera announced a gesture of good will for my Aunt Bernice. Bernice was one of a legion of retired English teachers in my family, living in a musty, old house that smelled of linoleum, cooking gas, and mildewed wooden siding. Barely able to make ends meet, Bernice was the occasional recipient of family charity. I know that my father paid her electric bill and sometimes my mother sent her a money order. She was a gentle woman who hid her embarrassment at these gifts with a wave of her hand.

"I have been intending to do something for Bernice," Vera began. "It's very difficult, I understand, to live on that small schoolteacher's pension. I sometimes wonder why she didn't work longer since the system would pay more if she had. It's such a burden," she continued, not revealing whether the object weighed more on Bernice or upon her. "In any case, I understand that her teeth are in terrible condition. One of my correspondents told me about it in a letter about six months ago. So I have arranged for her to visit the dentist at my expense. Up to and including dentures. I'm not sure where she got such weakness. My side of the family has always had strong bones and good health. Perhaps...but no matter. It's my gift to her." Vera re-straightened her back and looked at my mother sharply, as if challenging her to question the generosity of such an offer.

"That is very thoughtful of you, Vera," my mother began, quite unable to help herself. "But don't you think…the idea of offering to pay to…Well, yes, certainly, it is thoughtful of you. Have you told her?"

"No," said Vera, "I want it to be a surprise."

Somewhat later my mother filled in the ellipses of her reaction. "Can you imagine," she said, "offering to have someone's teeth pulled and considering that a gift? Anything else, especially money, would have been so much more thoughtful. Vera's gifts always have such dire consequences!"

I had no idea then that Vera's path and mine would cross again or that we would actually become friends of sorts. I rarely went home again after the first few summers in Chicago, and those visits never coincided with Vera's yearly descent. But after graduation I found my first job in Washington, DC, at a research firm that specialized in political consulting. For no particular reason other than the inconvenience it avoided, I did not call her or try to visit. There was no reason for her to know that I lived only a few miles from her house in one of the older Maryland suburbs. Washington was in 1970 still a conglomeration of small, provincial towns surrounding a provincial city; cut into wedges of segregated societies, with certain neighborhoods that extended out into similar suburban communities. So the embassies in Georgetown implied mansions on Reservoir Road, government employees congregating in the liberal agencies of the federal government commuted to Montgomery County, and military employees from the Pentagon crowded into the small garden apartments of Arlington, Virginia, while huge swaths of the city to the east and south were occupied by blacks who made up the manual laborers, maids, and lower-level federal employees. I managed to find an apartment in the city near my office, so I suspected I would probably never visit the area near the National Institutes of Health where Vera now lived—perhaps because Ralph had worked there.

Nonetheless, one rainy December evening, when I arrived home damp from the hasty walk from my office, the telephone rang. There was no mistaking her stern, clear voice.

"It's rude, don't you think, not to call your own relatives?" she began.

"Well, Vera," I mumbled, intending to make an apology, "what a surprise!"

"No doubt. Manners being what they are today. But this can't be the way you were raised."

"I'm sorry. I've been very busy with moving," I continued. "It's such a strange place, like no city I've ever seen before."

"It is that," she agreed. "Which is why I'm calling you. I am sure you will need some guidance here, some way to meet the right people. It's no good to try that on your own. That's what kinfolks are for."

"Quite kind of you, but..."

"No, definitely not kind. It's what I feel obligated to do. So, on Sunday next week, in the afternoon, I'm having a small party for you to get acquainted. I've invited several people you need to meet, from George Washington University and some other places in town. The right people with the sorts of connections you can use."

"That's extraordinarily nice of you, Cousin Vera, but my job isn't really about social connections. I'm really like a lawyer's clerk, a researcher, and a historian rolled into one."

"Fine," she interjected. "You be here at four. I've mailed you instructions—your mother was obliging with your address. And please dress properly. It is a Sunday. Just keep your church clothes on."

There was no mistaking the irony in her voice because she knew that church was the last place I would find myself on an early Sunday morning. "I'll be there," I responded.

"Well, then, good-bye. No need to linger on the telephone." I heard the click of the receiver.

That Sunday came quickly. I dressed in a dark work suit despite the promise of a thaw and took a cab to the Bethesda address she had sent to me. Her house was tidy and prim, expressing a neatness and care that protested against the adjoining yards with their evidences of children and dogs and untended gardens. Walking up the mossy brick porch steps, I knocked with the brass ring and heard it give a somber, deep-throated thud within. Vera opened the door and ushered me quickly into a living room crowded with antique furniture, lamps, tables, and intricate needlepoint set in picture frames around the walls. There were several couples talking softly and concentrating, it appeared, on balancing fragile teacups and paper-thin dinner plates with small, white-bread, crustless sandwiches in either hand. It would be a test of manners to converse at the same time. Vera introduced me to each couple in turn, indicating, in a word or two, just how each could help me enter the proper social circle or perhaps find a better place to live than downtown Washington. I had the sense throughout, however, that these were actually Vera's friends—that they knew, as well as I did, that I wanted to be on my own and that there were really no right social circles or proper addresses to learn.

Toward the end of the party, when all of the sandwiches had disappeared from paper doilies on the etched silver platter and the tea urn had turned cold, one of the women, Andrea Logan, pulled me aside. She was a generation younger than Vera and a former neighbor. Now living in Silver Spring, she had known Vera for almost ten years. "She's a wonderful character," she confided. "I've never met anyone quite as complicated. With such an amazing sense of humor. You know that she invited you today to meet her friends, her Washington family. That's the most important thing to her—relations—and she manages to make everyone feel as if they have some filial obligation to her. Look around this room. Everything here belonged to someone else: those antique dining chairs, the cut glass lamp base, even the needlepoint work. She has a story about each possession. She has also told me many times that your family doesn't appreciate her. Yet her house is a museum of artifacts from the Illinois aunts and uncles and cousins. You might even find some memento referring to you here. And, of course, you know about her niece?"

"No, not really. Not much," I replied to her last query, avoiding any commentary on her inventory of family things. "No one ever talks about her, least of all Vera. I only suspect—my whole family does—that something happened."

"Yes," she continued, dismissing the chance to reveal what it was. "I think it's a compensation of sorts—this house and this room. Vera really wants to belong to a family. Perhaps she would even move back to Southern Illinois, but her pride or her shame—however you want to put it—won't let her. You should be her friend."

I dismissed the temptation to comment on the potential depopulation of the southern half of the state were Vera to announce such a move. And yet I became, to some degree, the friend that Andrea Logan had proposed. I saw Vera every few months or so and found what her friends valued most in her: a profound sense of irony, an ability to laugh at her own rigidity. Even at her most serious moments of disapproval, as she clucked over some shocking breach of decorum recounted to her in a letter from home or a news story in the hometown newspaper, of which she remained a loyal and meticulous reader and noted typographical mistakes and bad grammar along with the public troubles of the community. It turned out also that she had several regular correspondents, including my mother, who related the latest family gossip. In fact, I began to suspect that Vera's unpopularity back home—her ability to make the family scatter when her visits portended—was because she knew too much. Recounted in long exchanges that must have been something like letters and responses to an advice-column writer, nothing of consequence in the family passed beneath her notice or beyond her impulse to give chastening advice. At the same time, her interference, like the gifts she sometimes tried to bestow on me—some discarded family possessions that she insisted I ought to treasure—seemed more to require a promise than a simple appreciation. Vera meant well, perhaps, but her gifts always came wrapped in the possibility of moral reform, the correction of behavior or an unspoken obligation.

One person Vera did not ever mention was her California niece, although I knew that the two exchanged greetings around those obligatory dates like birthdays and religious holidays that Vera would never allow to pass unrecognized. Whatever had led to their break, I knew that Vera found herself beyond even offering advice. And once when I asked, she looked away, as if distracted by some memory. She often repeated a sentence that had the sound of rationalization: "Abigail has her own life. She made her own choices."

It was about five years after I moved to Washington that I received a call in the early evening from Andrea Logan.

"I'm afraid I have bad news for you," she said quickly. "Vera is very ill… in the Washington Hospital Center…I've just visited her, and she wants you to come and make the arrangements. I'm still here at the hospital, but do get here as quickly as you can."

I took a cab across town to the hospital, arriving only about forty-five minutes later. Before I could enter her room, the attending nurse, who seemed to be waiting for me just outside, asked me to see the doctor first. His office was a glassed-in booth at the end of the corridor. I knocked, and he motioned me in.

"You are Vera's nephew," he began. "Her closest relation in the area?"

"Yes," I said. "Although she has a niece in California who should be informed."

"What you need to know," he continued, "is the prognosis, or rather the lack of it. She has had a very serious heart attack. The next one will probably be fatal. It could happen at any time."

"I'll see her immediately, then," I said and made a motion toward the door. But he held up his hand.

"This is an unusual case. I've known Vera for many years. Her husband Ralph was also my patient. So I understand something about her and the family. You should know that she is conscious now and asked specifically to see you. She seems to have all sorts of plans and instructions. She even asked her neighbor to bring over a copy of her will so she could show it to you."

"OK, Doctor. I'll go right now." I turned and walked back down the hallway over a floor that squeaked as my shoes scudded on its waxed surface. I knocked gently at the door and entered. Andrea, sitting at her bedside, jumped up as if very anxious to leave.

"You two have a great deal to discuss. I'll be back in the morning, Vera. Sleep well, dear…We all love you." She lightly touched Vera's hands and then turned, pushing carefully through the door, which closed with a snap behind her.

Vera lay propped up in the hospital bed, the sheet wrapped tightly around her frail body. Both hands, oversize next to her diminished wrists and arms, were linked across her stomach. Her eyes were closed, and her hair, coming loose from the stays that normally held it, flowered in confused swirls against the white pillow.

"Sit down," she said in a calm but weak voice. "I have a great deal to tell you before it's too late. I should have done this sooner."

"No, Vera," I blurted out. "I'm really sorry. Maybe we can put this off for when you're feeling better."

"But I won't ever be better," she said, opening her eyes. "Didn't you talk to that doctor? He told me the truth; I demanded it. Didn't he tell you?" I nodded in reply. "Well, here is what you need to do. First, call Abigail and tell her. No need to bother about convincing her to come. She wouldn't anyway. And then there is my will. I want you to read it because it's complicated. So you will know."

Vera took a number of short, difficult breaths and then pointed a finger at the folder on the nightstand. "There."

"I certainly will call. Maybe she will come. She ought to."

"And there is my obituary for the hometown paper. I wrote it several years ago, but nothing is changed. I am who I have always been. Make sure you place it. There's also a picture."

THE GIFT

I picked up the folder and found several items: a sheet with Abigail's address and phone number, the obituary, two carefully handwritten letters, a faded photograph, and the typed will folded inside a blue cover.

"No, she'll never come as long as I'm alive, and you should know why. It's not a long story, although no one in the family knows all the details. I've kept it from them. In any case, she may be glad to know about my condition."

"Oh, no. That can't possibly be, Vera. No one wants someone to…"

"Die," Vera corrected my lapse. "But there is the money, and she will certainly want that. It seems that I'm the only one in the whole family who can ever tell the truth. That's why they don't like me," she said. Then she moved her slight body with effort, and I wondered for an instant if the bedclothes were too tight.

"Shall I call the nurse?" I asked.

"Of course not," she replied. Then she began her story, which she told in short bursts of energy. "Even if I do feel badly, there isn't much time…Now, about Abigail, and please don't stop me! We had a terrible disagreement when she was fifteen. Abigail was a wild teenager. She got involved with the wrong sort of boys and wouldn't stop. I took her to a doctor and the minister of our church after the high school counselor told me about the gossip she had overheard. Abigail was a…I still can't bring myself to say the word. I warned her. I even told her some things I knew about her mother and father in hopes she would avoid their mistakes, but she just glared at me, sullen and stubborn. But I couldn't have a scandal. An unwanted pregnancy, for example. A forced marriage to someone who would destroy her life. So I locked her up. Not literally, of course, but I made sure that she went to school and then came home right afterwards. She wasn't allowed to have boyfriends, to receive telephone calls, or to go anywhere but to church or to visit with me. Maybe I was too strict, but what would I have told the family? I couldn't bear the disgrace. Why couldn't she wait? And then, one day, she simply left and never spoke to me again. I only have an address and a phone number that I've never called. I have no ideas what she has become. Except that I found out she has two children."

Seemingly due to the effort required of giving this long account, Vera closed her eyes and sank further into the embrace of the bed.

"What should I do, then?" I asked. "Isn't it possible that she's forgiven you?"

64

"Forgive me? Nonsense. There is nothing to forgive," Vera insisted abruptly. "Do you know? Even when I make a gesture. The closer people are to you, the more they expect and the less they appreciate. But I want to give Abigail another chance. If you read the will, you'll see what I mean."

I opened the crisp pages and skimmed quickly. There were small bequests to her church and several charities, with one long section leaving the bulk of her estate to two individuals whose names I did not recognize.

"It's a good deal of money, you'll see," Vera broke in. "Ralph and I saved everything. Perhaps, with the house, it's worth a million dollars."

"And you are leaving most of it to two strangers?"

"Not quite," she said weakly. "Those two are Abigail's children. They must be sixteen and seventeen now—just about the age when she left me. I couldn't control Abigail, even though I tried to guide her in the right direction, show her the proper way. So the money couldn't possibly pass directly to her, even though she must assume that it will, but to her two children. It will be held in trust until they are both at least twenty-one, and then it will be divided between them."

"But that means that you've cut her out entirely. Maybe because she left—that's understandable—but you couldn't know the children at all. What they are like."

"On the contrary," she interrupted, her voice momentarily regaining its usual timbre. "You see, when the two children, Benjamin and Sandra, reach twenty-one, they will each get a letter from me along with their inheritance. You have copies in the file. I've provided both with a carefully written family history, and I also set aside money to keep several family things in storage until they can claim them if they want. At the end of their letters, I have explained what I hope they will do. If Abigail has been a good mother—and I have no idea at all—if she has raised them properly, if she has returned to the family tradition and taught them good manners and obligations, then they will follow my request. I have asked them each to give her two hundred thousand dollars. It's a generous gift to an estranged kinsman."

"But, Vera," I interjected, "you don't know them at all. You don't know if they love or hate their mother. And twenty-one is such a selfish age. Wouldn't it be better to give her something for sure? To forgive her."

THE GIFT

Vera opened her eyes very wide. In the fluorescent light, I noticed the hectic blemishes on her face and arms. It was suddenly a very distressing moment, and I wanted to leave.

And then she spoke again, this time more faintly. "No, I want to give a gift that means something, to give someone something that they will appreciate but also something they will receive only if they deserve it. Maybe—maybe—she's changed, and she'll get the gifts; maybe her children will share with her." Vera closed her eyes, and her silence pronounced an end to our talk. I picked up the papers and opened the door.

"I'll visit you tomorrow, Vera," I said.

But there was no response. I waited a moment and then turned and walked out into the hallway, whose vivid fluorescent light, gleaming on the polished floor and walls, shone with the glare of a false, antiseptic healing.

THE DIARY

My memories of that place of origins, after thirty years, return in broken shards—glimmering pieces of sounds and smells that still manage to suggest extraordinary impressions without ever quite revealing why. How else to explain the sharp pang of emotion created by the vivid recollection of that shabby front porch with its squeaky wooden swing? Or the dark, decaying, long wall of the living room covered in faded wallpaper or the metallic ticking of the railroad clock over the mantle? Or the pervasive smell of kitchen linoleum impregnated by a century of cooking gas and splattered grease?

When my grandfather was still alive, he sat in front of the massive black-and-white television screen for hours, tin ear horn tilted toward the sound, which was turned up so loud that it distorted the words beyond recognition; he was always trying to catch the play-by-play of the St. Louis Cardinals baseball games. Nothing could persuade him to wear a hearing aid or turn down the sound, for an outsize vanity made him deny his loss of hearing. My grandmother, a sullen, quiet woman, who was always dressed in a floral housecoat and scarcely spoke to us when we appeared, would only occasionally and briefly emerge from her room.

I also remember Sunday meals and other special occasions like Easter honored by the doubling of every dish, served on a thick linen tablecloth with chunky silverware. There were always two kinds of meat, usually chicken and ham, as well as sweet potatoes, green beans in bacon and vinegar, broccoli, two salads of wilted lettuce and coleslaw, and several pies and cakes, all spread out in silver and glass dishes on the sideboard. The redundancy only prolonged the meals and emphasized the long silences at the table.

Waiting outside on the porch for dinner were some of the longest minutes of my childhood—the to-and-fro of the swing like a slow-motion pendulum measuring my impatience. Inside, my mother and father talked to a varying array of elderly aunts with stark white hair and rice paper skin and who smelled of powder and lipstick. On those long, quiet, sweltering afternoons, I believed that time had never granted this dreary, old railroad town a youth, that it was built new with an already-dying square, supplied from the beginning with dusty stores and an ancient railroad switching line that backed almost into my grandfather's backyard. Even the cars speeding down East Main Street, their tires slapping the broken brick pavement, clattered like ancient carts or wagons hurrying by. Everything, like my family and aunts and uncles, was old and decaying.

Most curious was the figure of my Aunt Blanche, a high school English teacher who continued to live in the old house with my grandparents. Like a boarder or a guest who knows she has stayed too long, she spent long periods in her room. When she emerged, she scarcely spoke to her father or mother. Whatever truce that existed between them had never been negotiated by openly spoken words; its terms were conceived and sealed in silence. Only an occasional sharp look or a nod of disapproval suggested her unhappiness.

With visiting nieces and nephews, she communicated largely by correcting our egregious grammatical errors. A particularly awful mistake sometimes provoked her to compare us to the students she taught, the sullen daughters and sons of the surrounding agricultural community. On occasions we thought we overheard a snatch of her internal dialogue, a blurted-out sound that suddenly and piecemeal broke through her silences—the habit of a lonely, solitary person who is the best and only audience for her secret thoughts.

One secret, I think, was that she drank. Never to excess, of course, but also never in public, and because of this, her secret habit suggested the furtive gestures of an alcoholic. Sometimes I could smell the sweetness of sherry on her breath. Everyone knew and no one cared about this clandestine habit, but the pretense allowed her to reject, with a cluck of disapproval, the strong mixed drinks that my grandfather and my parents occasionally seemed to enjoy.

Aunt Blanche was a stocky, buxom woman with carrot-red hair, dyed in memory of the glorious childhood amber that I never saw but that my mother told me had made her a beauty many years before. I only saw the brassy substitute, the finger curls of dyed orange, rolled so tight that they let pale patches of white, gleaming scalp shine through between them.

There never was an "uncle" associated with her, nor, of course, any cousins. Like several of the elderly women in my family, she never married. In fact, I could never imagine her as anything other than an elderly aunt whose stern looks and strict lectures seemed designed to dampen the happiness of any children she met. I thought they were nothing to her other than future pupils who would require correction.

I was not surprised or very much upset when she began an abrupt decline many years later, after my grandparents had passed. As my mother's only sibling, she had become a distant fixture in my life; I rarely saw her since I was at graduate school doing an American history degree. I didn't know the cause of her death immediately—I had only received letters from my mother marking the progress of her illness. But I hoped she might leave something in her will for my mother, who needed it, and so I asked about that when she called to describe the funeral.

"Did Blanche leave you anything?"

"Yes, I suppose so. A small savings account and the proceeds of the house sale, which isn't worth very much. I'll have to go down and clean it out. Most of the furniture is too old to sell, so I'll probably give it to her church. There's some silver and china, but beyond that…"

"Isn't there anything else?" I asked. I was fishing for some mention of the diary I thought Aunt Blanche had kept.

"Not really…just a few personal things."

"Mom, wasn't there a diary? Didn't you tell me once about a diary?"

"Well, yes, I think there is. But Blanche gave specific instructions in her will to destroy it, and I intend to."

"What kind of diary? You know something like that sounds very valuable to a historian," I answered. "What years does it cover?"

"I believe she began sometime around the end of World War I—she was only about ten then. And as far as I know, she was still making entries up to the last year or so. That makes about sixty years."

Suddenly I became very interested. "Why not save it for me to look at? A document like that would be a wonderful historical source—growing up and growing old in a little Illinois town in those crucial middle years of the century: the twenties, the Depression, the postwar decline. I'd like to know how the world appeared to her. It might be worth an article or even a book of some sort."

After a pause, my mother explained firmly, "Oh, I couldn't let you see it, historian or not."

"Why? What could be so secret?"

Again she paused. "I don't want to tell you. Except that Blanche did something when she was young that she was ashamed of…of which she was ashamed," she corrected herself, remembering Blanche's dislike of dangling prepositions. "So she instructed me to burn the diaries."

THE DIARY

"I'll tell you what. Why not look them over and see what's in them? If it's OK, in your opinion, maybe you could save them for me to look at. After all, I'm not interested in scandal, just what life must have been like to such a woman living so long in such a place. You could even tear out some of the pages if you think they are embarrassing."

"All right," she promised, "I'll read the diaries and let you know. But I'm not hopeful for your sake."

Since it was nearing the Christmas season, I decided to go home for the holidays to Chicago, where my mother lived. I also planned to make a personal appeal to her to preserve the diaries at least until I could read them.

Thinking about my trip, I hoped to enlist my sister in the plan. But she was not happy about my request or sanguine about what our mother would decide.

"You know, you pry," she told me in a telephone conversation. "It seems to be your nature."

"Oh, no," I answered, "it's in my profession. We have to ask questions. That's how we understand what happened in the past."

"Don't fabricate," she exclaimed. "You're only a historian in the first place because you like to know secrets and gossip. It gives you a license to invade the privacy of the dead. Whatever happened to you? I remember as a child you were only happy when you were by yourself."

"That's probably why: history was my cure—reaching out to people who couldn't answer back. Now curiosity is my profession."

"Still a vicarious way to live, though," she exclaimed. "In the end, you take after Aunt Blanche. You probably even keep a diary of your own, if I know you."

"No," I answered, "but I really want to read hers."

"Don't be disappointed," she said and hung up.

I flew to Chicago two days later, not quite knowing what to expect. On the bus trip from the airport, I was impressed (as always) by the flat sameness of the landscape and then the endless clusters of suburbs and strip malls. I had grown up near here; I had lived without mountains; and my youthful travels to Southern Illinois had all been on straight highways lined by precise rows of corn and wheat and that passed through small towns with one or two stoplights to impede the flow of traffic. The tidiness and lack of variation of this physical world was, nonetheless, always comforting because it placed no demands upon the soul; it squelched worrisome ambitions. It was a horizon of limited possibilities. "What could Aunt Blanche have possibly done," I thought, "that could be so scandalous, so imaginative that she could not bear to let it live beyond her days? And why didn't she destroy the diary herself? And why did she never leave home?"

My mother greeted me at the door of her apartment. I hung up my hat and coat and wandered into the living room. "Are you hungry?" she asked in a tone that indicated she had prepared a special meal for me.

"Yes, sure, I'm always hungry," I said.

"Sit down at the table. Everything is just about ready," she called as she moved quickly into the kitchen.

This was typical of our relationship. My comings and goings were ignored. When I was present, my mother became my mother again, cooking, washing, and doing the hundreds of other useful things for someone else that she had become skilled in throughout a life of waiting on others.

We sat down at a table in a corner of the living room.

"I just can't get used to eating in the living room," she said. "Ever since your father died and I had to move, I've had to make do with this arrangement. I think that the most painful part of growing old is losing the rooms you live in. One by one they disappear. First the dining room, then the kitchen, then the living room, and finally all you have left is a dreary bed in a nursing home, a curtain around you, and no privacy."

"You shouldn't talk that way, Mom," I said. "It's just Aunt Blanche's death that has you thinking like that." I helped myself to mashed potatoes, pot roast, and green beans. "You've made a Southern Illinois dinner, Mom," I exclaimed when I tasted the bacon and vinegar on the beans.

"I should have gone back," she said. "I could have lived with Blanche; I could have been there to help her."

"But the whole town is dead. What would you do? I'm sure the family is mostly gone. Anyone young enough to put one foot in front of the other has fled. And living in that old, musty house next to the railroad tracks! Chicago has to be better than that."

"Certainly, it's better," she agreed.

Now that we had edged up to the subject, I thought I should finally ask. "Well, what about the diary? Was it there? Did you read it?"

"Oh, yes," she nodded, "it was where she always kept it, in the bedroom, in the drawer of her dressing table, tied up in a pink ribbon."

I remembered as a child sneaking into my aunt's room. What I thought I wanted to discover there was never clear to me. I was drawn to the mystery of this elderly woman who seemed to have no obvious life and so many secrets. But there was nothing to discover. Just a few boxes and tubes on the pink-skirted makeup table in front of an oval mirror that bore traces of missing silver around the edges. On her dresser was a large Bible with a scuffed cover and a red ribbon place mark. And at a writing desk, there were neat piles of student-exam books and precisely arranged pencils and pens. The only surprise was a canopied bed, draped, like so much else, in pink with an edging of white ruffles. The ensemble made me uncomfortable, and I always left quickly. Her room was as blank and uncommunicative as the profile of the person she was willing to show to us.

"So," I said. "Did you find the passages Blanche was worried about?"

"Yes, they were there."

"Well, don't keep me in suspense. What did you do with the diary?"

"I burned it, just like she told me to," she said sternly. "It took me a long time because the flue in the fireplace wasn't working properly."

"But, Mom, why? You know I wanted to see it. How could anything matter now? A dead town, an exhausted and completed life, no relatives left to speak of. What in the world did she do that was so awful?"

"You don't understand, Son."

"No, I certainly don't. What happened? Can you tell me?"

"Certainly, I can; I certainly don't mind. When Blanche was about twenty-two, just out of college and beginning her teaching in high school, she fell in love with the local minister of the Baptist church. You know she was very beautiful in those days. Everyone thought she would marry well, although I was surprised she didn't leave town. Why she went back, after college, I don't know. Except, of course, she wanted to protect Granddad."

"What a horrible reason! He was the last person who needed protection, and anyway, he married Grandma!"

"Blanche did it anyway, moving back into her room in the old house where she could keep an eye on them. And then she met the minister. Of course, he was married and had two children. His wife was the choir soloist and taught Sunday school. They were a very active pair. They ran the whole church themselves: Tuesday prayer meetings, a youth group, charity drives. But Blanche fell in love, and so did he, and eventually, they had an affair."

"You mean they had sex, Mom. I can hardly believe it of Blanche!"

"Yes, the affair went on for almost a year, and she recorded every part of it in the diary."

"But I don't understand," I exclaimed. "What happened then?"

"Well, finally, Blanche decided that she had to call it off. There was no chance for them to be together, and so she just quit seeing him. In fact, she joined a different church, the Methodists, just to cut ties with him."

"But," I asked, "if it went on for a year, surely someone else in town must have known about it?"

"Yes, indeed," said my mother. "Everyone knew about it. You can't prevent rumors in a small town."

"Then I'm completely puzzled. What on earth made you burn a diary that recounts an affair ended so long ago? Why did you have to destroy it if everyone knew anyway?"

"Oh, no, you just don't understand," she said. "How could she confess to the world a secret that she had lived forty years to protect? Letting anyone else read her own words would have been an excruciating confession; and that would make the scandal unbearably real. Would give it a new life."

AMIMAL SNAP

The school bus lumbered to a stop in front of his house. The familiar driver leaned over and pulled the spindle-hinged handle, and the double doors folded open with a swish. Bill mumbled a brief hello as he clambered up the two steps and then turned to look down the half-filled aisle to find a seat. The bus jerked forward, its low gear straining and moaning. There were several empty rows, and he chose a middle one and slid down the bench. Taking off his gloves, he slid his fingers along the cold iron railing of the seat in front. The leatherette seat covering was still chilly and colored a dark brown, and it made no noise as he moved across it. Grit and sand crunched under his feet as he settled in. The familiar smell of orange peels and melting snow hung in the air as well as the chatter of the other riders. How extraordinary it would be next year when he could drive to school. Sixteen was the dividing age between being entirely dependent and truly becoming oneself, he felt. If only it were possible to speed time up and reach that point now. Then life might really begin. But until then he had to endure the indignity of being only fifteen. He would know in the next year or at least certainly not much later than that. He would make some sort of decision once and for all and live with it for the rest of his life, never turning back. Everything else would be in the past like his first fifteen years.

The bus lurched along in high gear to the next stop, which was Stephen's. He was sure to be there today as always. He was one of those friends whose voice had deepened first. His blond hair was now darker, as if he had suddenly turned somber and adult, and a stubble of beard appeared in shadows on his face on those days he forgot to shave. Before then, he had been cute, or so the girls in his class had told him, but now he was handsome, with broadening shoulders and a slower, almost-rolling stride. He always wore Levi's, some sort of bright, fresh dress shirt, and a white undershirt that sometimes rode up above the highest button. Other boys were beginning to experiment with styles, following the newest fashions in haircuts or boots or belts. But Stephen was always crisp-looking, casual in an effortless way that no one else seemed quite able to emulate.

When the school bus stopped, several students and then Stephen hopped in.

"Sit here, Steve," he shouted, waving an arm in greeting and indicating the empty space next to him. Stephen sat down next to him, banging his feet against the footrest to loosen the snow on his cuffs and shoes.

"Another really cold one," he exclaimed, hugging Bill as if to pretend this would make it warmer. His body was cold from the outside air, but his touch shot through Bill like a bolt. He responded by pressing his leg slightly against Stephen's, and although Stephen did not attempt to move, the intensity of the contact suddenly drained.

The bus plowed on, stopping every few blocks until it was about half a mile from the school. Stephen suddenly got up and shuffled to the back of the bus, sliding in beside two girls from a higher class. They were soon engaged in an animated conversation, bobbing their heads in agreement. Bill looked intently at Stephen, trying to send a message to call him back. Bill wanted, somehow, to bring up the subject of the sweet-sixteen party Stephen was having Saturday night. Everyone knew about it, even those who had no expectation of being invited. But for some reason—maybe the mail hadn't come yet, or maybe Stephen had just forgotten—no one had said anything to Bill about it. But he was sure he would be asked and that Stephen would sponsor him in the club of the most popular boys in the class. Stephen was already a member and a good friend, and Bill knew that was exactly what good friends were for. It was common knowledge that there were still two openings and the new members would be initiated on Saturday night. He tried again, pouring as much energy as he could into his gaze, knowing that he could make it happen. There was nothing magic here or telepathic—it just seemed that he could control a situation or bend an outcome if he really wanted to, if he wished with all his might and focused his pure energy into a look or an imagined outcome. But Stephen seemed not to notice, although as he piled out with the other students, he paused for a minute to glance in Bill's direction.

Bill wondered if he had felt the message, if he could really project feelings this way...the way he could control himself. If Stephen invited him, he promised himself, if he paid attention this one last time, he would be able to forget the strange feelings he had and finally push them deep down inside himself and out of sight forever. Hidden there they would surely be invisible to anyone else... his mother...his sisters...even his father. He couldn't even remember when it had begun: the game of controlling the frightening emotions he sometimes felt. He had learned to bury them in obscure places where no one suspected their presence and where he could forget them most of the time. And if he sometimes vaguely felt their presence, he could convince himself that they all existed in the past of someone else: not him. They were the way he used to feel and think, not what he would become.

Yet there was one memory among them that he sometimes allowed himself. That was the special time when Stephen had slept overnight about a year ago. This was a time he would never want to purge, and when it came back to him in a hot flash, he held on to the picture in his mind, concentrating all his senses and reliving each moment again until he was exhausted and the intensity finally faded. Some of the unimportant details were forgotten…like why Stephen had spent the night. And so he invented the reasons as a way to extend the pleasure and complete the story. Perhaps they spent a long night watching television together; maybe they had an intense conversation about the future—college, ambitions, cars, girls—and they probably had a serious talk about the superficiality of life in the suburbs and the narrow lives of their parents. When they had finally gone to bed, Bill never slept or only slept fitfully, feeling every motion of Stephen's body, listening to him inhale and exhale and slowing his own breathing to the same cadence. Occasionally, he carefully moved closer, touching Stephen's body with his arm or shoulder or thigh, thinking and hoping that he, too, was awake and wondering if he had the same feelings. Bill could play with this memory again and again, rewriting the story of how it began and daring to guess how it might have ended. And then in the morning, when the sun came pouring into the bedroom and it was impossible to pretend to sleep anymore, they would wake up…with no words passing between them and no recognition of the closeness of their bodies or the dreamy intimacy that had stretched throughout the night. This jewel in the black velvet box of his memory, hidden most of the time even from himself, was to be retrieved only for special occasions. He only allowed himself this one exception by promising that it would never happen again. He would find the strength to go on and transform himself into something different.

This memory raced through his mind so quickly that he could not recall why he had allowed it to surface or what made him think of it as he trudged up the front steps of the high school. It was a strange, pretentious building with a looming ziggurat tower over the entrance and odd, angular windows, doorways, and hall ceilings inside, as if the architect had been struck by lightning and could only design in thunderbolts, never missing the opportunity to employ a zigzag when a straight line or a square corner would do. Bright murals in angular frames around the entranceway depicted heavily muscled men assaulting bulky machinery with wrenches and hammers, adding to the impression that this building had been constructed purposely to show off the arcane symbols and dizzying passageways to some sort of mysterious or dangerous adulthood.

As they scuffed and skidded over the slippery floor, already wet from the passage of boots and dripping jeans, toward their lockers and then their first classes, he thought perhaps he should mention to Stephen that he hadn't received an invitation to the party yet and that probably, for whatever reason, it hadn't come. He was sure he could find some way to broach the subject, some nonchalant and vague way to start the conversation. Perhaps before lunch when they went to retrieve their sandwiches and before the crush and crowds of the lunchroom, he could find the right moment.

Later, after the bell that ended Creative Writing class, he quickly gathered up his books and hurried to his locker, where he thought he might catch Stephen for an unguarded moment. When he arrived, Stephen was rummaging around for his brown lunch bag. Seeing him from the back, Bill noticed once again the curve of his Levi's, which tightened around his hips and then hung loose around his long legs. His shirt was white with broad green and brown stripes that crossed over his broad shoulders front and back. Bill stopped and gazed at him for a moment until he turned around slowly.

"Hey, Bill," he exclaimed. "How was English? Are you still writing those fantasies? You must have a hundred collected by now. What an imagination. But I guess it takes that to pass that class. I hear that Miss Turnbull is great, if you can get onto her good side. I was thinking next year I might try it. I'm getting really tired of math and science. I should take some of those softer courses, you know, with more girls in them…like you do."

Bill blushed and then recovered, saying, "Yes, you should try it if you want to meet girls. That's the place…and French class especially. There are only three guys out of twenty. That makes seven apiece," he said with bravado.

"Well, I'll leave the *parlez-vous* to you," Stephen said with a wink and started to close his locker. "Probably peanut butter if I can predict it, with a banana of course," he exclaimed, slamming the flimsy door with a metallic shudder. "Unless my mother got creative, which I seriously doubt. Do you want to trade?"

"Wait a minute," Bill said, jerking open his locker and pulling out his sandwich bag. "No, peanut butter here, too. Although sometimes my mom puts homemade jelly on it."

"No, thanks, then," said Stephen, turning to leave.

Bill stopped him with a light touch to the arm. "Something I wanted to ask you…it's not important, but just while I thought of it."

"Sure," said Stephen.

"I was wondering if you'd like to come over Saturday night. I think my parents are going out of town, and we could watch TV. Or listen to a couple of the new records I just bought. Stay the night," Bill added, almost inaudibly.

Stephen looked at him strangely for a second and then relaxed. He started to speak but then hesitated, carefully choosing his words. "Well, thanks anyway. I don't think I can. I've got other plans that night."

"OK, fine," Bill said meekly. "Another time. I'll catch up to you in a minute. Go on ahead." As he turned away, a rush of embarrassment passed over him like a huge wave, and he feared he would reel and stagger under its blow. Why, he wondered, had he asked Stephen to spend the night? He had only intended to ask what he was doing on Saturday, but instead, this had come out! He had promised himself it would never happen again. And was that strange, momentary look that crossed Stephen's face some sort of signal that he had understood, that he, too, was thinking about that time a year ago…only differently? And why hadn't he mentioned the sweet-sixteen party, unless of course Bill wasn't invited and would never become part of that popular group of boys? He would never feel the rough-and-tumble physicality that they always exhibited when they greeted one another in the halls and at football and basketball games. Did Stephen suspect something about him? Did the others know, too? He would have to try harder to deny everything he felt, to cut out and "cauterize"—to use the new word he had just learned in writing class today—even obliterate that single, wonderful memory he treasured. Could he burn it out and stop it with a backfire brighter and more destructive and intense than its familiar warmth? He would have to try.

He paused for another moment and then hurried off to the lunchroom.

For the rest of the day, he felt a nagging embarrassment, as if he were on the edge of reliving or about to experience some terrible calamity. Were other students watching him, looking at him strangely? Did they notice? In fact, he was unusually distracted, and more than once he caught the inquisitive eye of one of his teachers who regularly depended upon his attention and participation. At about two o'clock, as he entered his last class, Miss LaSalle stopped him and handed him a yellow call slip, a permission to be out in the hall after the bell rang. Usually it was provided as a request to meet with another teacher or administrator. He quickly glanced at it but recognized neither the name—Miss Angel—nor the room number that was obviously located somewhere on the third-floor corridor of offices.

"Do you know what this is?" he asked his teacher cautiously.

"Not really," she said, "but you need to go. Don't worry about class. You can get the homework assignment from someone else."

He looked again at the call slip and, as the bell rang, opened the door and stepped out into the empty hallway. He walked along the polished linoleum floor to the staircase and then reluctantly climbed up, his shoes grating on the tread strips. At the top, he turned right and walked to the office, room 306. The wooden door was shut, but the wavy, opaque glass revealed a light and three shadowy figures. To the side of the doorway was a flat metal box with a glass opening. Behind it was a card on which was printed "Miss Angel, Speech Therapist." He hesitated, puzzled, wondering if this weren't some mistake. So he knocked very tentatively.

"Come in," responded a very musical voice.

He opened the heavy door and stepped inside, letting it close behind him. There were three people seated at a square table, with one empty chair. Two were other students—he recognized them but not the teacher, Miss Angel, who stood to greet him.

"I got this call slip," he said. "You wanted to see me about something?"

"Oh, yes, Bill," she said pleasantly. "Come in and sit down."

He pulled the chair back and half-slid into it, still not sure why he should be there and reluctant to settle in. He glanced at the other two students and then at Miss Angel. She was wearing a tight yellow angora sweater with large ivory buttons. Her hair was blond and firmly set into large curls that framed her head. He could smell a mixture of makeup and perfume, and he noticed that her carefully manicured hands had no rings. Her bare, chubby arms were blotched with faint freckles and covered in fuzzy, pale hair.

"This is a speech therapy class," she exclaimed, "and what we do here is to correct little problems of pronunciation that we might have. So many students need help, and, well…it's a good thing to catch these problems now, because in later life they can become a serious obstacle. Other people will notice them, and we don't want that, do we? It's distracting for one thing, and we always want everyone to listen to what we are saying and not how we say it."

"But I…" he interjected, "don't understand why…"

"Perhaps not," explained Miss Angel, "but about a month or so ago, I visited one of your classes. I usually stay in the back where no one will notice me. You were probably sitting in the front. I remember that you talked frequently and gave very smart answers, and I'm sure your teacher appreciated it. But I did detect a light…discernible…faint…lisp. And we'd like to work on that, wouldn't we?"

He flushed suddenly. "No, I don't think so. I mean, I never knew about it, never heard that…no one has ever said anything to me," he blurted out.

"Well, it's apparent," said Miss Angel with a sympathetic smile. "It's for your own good, of course, and you don't have to stay or even come back. But it would be very helpful if you could visit just once a week. You will make quick progress just like Bettina and Johnny here. I'm sure."

His initial blush faded into shame and then anger. "Could his friends detect a lisp?" he wondered. So many times when they were all kidding around, someone affected an exaggerated lisp to indicate a girl or worse. . Is that what they heard from him? Is that what Stephen heard? Is that why the sweet sixteen would never elect him to membership: his lisp? The possibility of this explanation was a horror that knocked down all his defenses and touched the very core of his self-control. Did everyone ridicule him behind his back? Did they imitate his slurred s's behind his back? He was seized by panic and the desire to run out of the room as fast as he could, but an even heavier emotion of shame weighed him down in his chair. He couldn't move.

"I'm so glad you came in today," continued Miss Angel, not noticing—or ignoring—the changing expressions that flared across his face. "Because we were just about to begin a game we frequently play. It's called animal snap. Quite simple, really. You pick up a card, and on the other side is a cartoon drawing of an animal or a bird or another object. You just make the noise of the animal or then say the name as carefully as you can, and if you pronounce everything properly, the card goes onto a pile next to the deck. If you have just a tiny problem, then you keep the card, and we will work on the sounds when we finish several rounds. Of course there aren't any winners, except everyone improves, and there is never, ever a loser. This is just to help. So, Johnny, why don't you start and show Bill how we play?"

Johnny looked at the deck and cautiously turned over the first card. He was a small boy with a somewhat frightened look and very large blue eyes. He gripped the card nervously, bending it from end to end while glancing at the animal. It looked as if he said "oh no" to himself.

"Remember to show us; don't be bashful," Miss Angel reminded him. And Johnny turned over the card, revealing a duck.

"Qua...qua...quack," he stammered.

"Very nice," intoned Miss Angel. "But I think you should take a deep breath before you say a word like that. It will relax you."

"...Quack!" he exclaimed.

"Very well done," said Miss Angel. "But I think we'll want to keep the card for later and the end of the game. Now your turn, Bettina."

Bettina looked unhappily at the pile. She was probably as reluctant to be here as Bill was. He thought he recognized her from the hallway. She was a pretty, dark-haired girl who often experimented with heavy and bright make-up, giving her a look that was both older and somewhat coarse. This and her tight sweaters and skirts invited comments from his friends, but he really didn't know much else about her.

Taking a card in her hand, she snapped it onto the table.

"Dat's a rabbit," she said, "and it don't make no noise unless you step on it or shoot it!"

Miss Angel laughed nervously. "Very good; I like that answer, but you do need to try again. Say 'th'—put your tongue toward the front of your mouth— 'that's a rabbit.'"

"Dat's a wabbit: 'squeak, squeak.'" Bettina repeated, defiantly smacking the card face down in front of her.

It was his turn, and he reached tentatively for a card. It was the picture of a coiled cobra.

"Cobra," he enunciated.

"Well, yes, of course," said Miss Angel, "but you need to tell us in general what sort of animal it is. Generic for cobra," she continued, adding a term to the game that would rule the choice of words.

82

"It's a snake," Bill answered, and without being prompted continued, "and the sound it makes is a *hithh*."

There, he had said it, and at the same time, he had heard it! For the first time ever, he realized that he did have a lisp. Slight but clearly audible. He turned bright red and felt tears forming in the corners of his eyes. He took his fingers and brushed them away as if he were merely clearing his vision.

"Hiss," said Miss Angel carefully. "When you say an *s*, move your tongue more to the back of your mouth and don't hold onto the sound. I think that will help."

"Hitthsss," he repeated.

"Well, let's keep that card for the end of the game, shall we?" she suggested. "Now let's go around again and on to the end now that you know how to play."

Each of them, in turn, picked up cards and snapped them down until finally the deck was exhausted.

"Dat's a lion: roar." "That's a chi…chi…chicken, and it goes ca…ca…ca…" "That's a mouth…mouse…and it goes squeak."

By the end of the hour, he was barely conscious of the room, Miss Angel, or the other two students. His ears were straining to hear the bell ring so he could escape. Several times, Miss Angel had to call him out of his reverie. But he did know one thing: he had already decided he could never come back. He could never bear the shame if anyone found out where he spent this awful hour or that he had a lisp.

On the long ride back home on the bus, Stephen leaned over from the seat behind him and asked, "What was the call slip about? Are you in trouble?" He said this ironically because, of course, Bill was never in trouble.

"Oh, no, just a committee they want me to be on, as student representative. Might get me out of some classes, too, if I accept."

"Oh," said Stephen, leaning back, apparently satisfied with the answer.

When he got home, he removed his boots and coat and went immediately up to his room to wait for dinner. He wanted to avoid the busy gossip of his sisters who sat in the kitchen watching his mother diligently prepare the meal. It was a Tuesday night, so he knew they would have roast chicken and potatoes and green beans…all his father's favorites. That meant he would be in a good mood, expansive and talkative even, despite his long day at the office and the crowded commuter train. He knew that his father actually liked these long rides. Sometimes he played a game of bridge when he and his friends could re-verse one of the train seats and play across the space in front of them…but he squirmed at the thought of cards and that horrible game of "animal snap" he had just endured. Shaking his head to rid his mind of the thought, he returned to focus on his father, who liked to tell hunting and fishing stories or discuss the trials of the always-floundering Chicago Bears and their ever-bleak prospects for the next season. He knew about these train rides because, once in a while, he accompanied his father to the city. He loved to listen to the sports stories, told in the warm glow of male camaraderie, where each of the men seemed to offer an opinion that everyone respected. He wondered if he would ever be-come comfortable in that way, *could* ever become like that, with a repertoire of stories and experiences and wisdom that others would accept. Would he ever be as natural and careless as they seemed, or was he doomed to calculate every thought and gesture…and now every sound…he made?

Tonight his father arrived punctually at 6:30, throwing open the door to let in a column of cold air from the outside. He could hear the door slam shut and the commotion and murmured voices as his father stepped inside, stamping the remaining snow off his shoes and greeting his mother and sisters.

"Bill…everyone…dinner," his mother called after a while, and he waited a few minutes and then reluctantly got out of the armchair where he had been ab-sently trying to read a book. He made his way silently down the carpeted stairs. As he entered the dining room, both his mother and father looked up at him, a sure sign that they had been discussing him. No doubt his mother had said something. She could always sense when something had gone wrong when he came home from school silent and unresponsive and took to his room with a book. Usually in afternoons he sat in the kitchen with her while she made dinner, watching the elaborate work it took to prepare a meal. Or sometimes, just for fun, he teased his sisters until the ruckus earned each of them a household task. But tonight was different, and he knew his mother had detected something unusual.

All five of them sat down to the long Maple wood table, already set with place mats, silver, glasses, and napkins with three large bowls, serving spoons, and a pile of plates in front of his father, who sat at the head. His mother perched on her chair close to the kitchen door, ready to fetch some extra dish or condi-ment or drink.

His two sisters sat at either side of his mother, while he was placed closest to his father, even though he was the oldest. It was an unspoken family rule: it was always men against women, male versus female, whether at the table, driving in the car, or walking in a group, when he and his father were always in the front.

His father liked to serve them; the bowls were never passed until the end of the meal. Why he did this was something of a quirk...or a mystery. But Bill had decided that his father wanted to establish himself as the source of this bounty, as the breadwinner, although it was really his mother and now also his sisters, who were beginning to learn the skills of cooking and housekeeping, who made it possible.

Tonight his father served with obvious relish and gave Bill an extra amount. There was silence as they fell to eating, although his father always complimented his mother. His two sisters began a conversation across the table about a new movie they wanted to see, and his mother joined in on the plans. He was scarcely aware of what they were saying.

Suddenly, his father turned to him with a look of sympathy that he realized was premeditated. Serious conversations always began this way, with his knowing that his father had prepared a brief speech.

"So, how was school today, Bill? What did you learn?" he began.

"OK. Nothing much," he said, trying to control the questioning by giving as brief an answer as possible and hoping his father would quickly tire of this feckless conversation.

But he persisted. "Well, something must have happened...good or bad... it always does. Are all your classes OK? Still making good grades?"

"Yes," he responded.

"That's not much of an answer," he father retorted, his voice rising slightly. "You'll have to do better than that when I ask you a perfectly normal question!"

Now he was sure that his mother had said something; somehow she had recognized his unhappiness, or maybe she had seen the residue of tears on his cheeks or noticed the slump in his shoulders left from his encounter with Miss Angel and Stephen. He blushed as the sounds of that terrible game came back to him.

"So what happened to you? Why are you acting this way...so silent?" his father persisted. "Look at me!"

"It was horrid," he burst out. "It was a horrid day."

But as he started to explain the reasons, his father interrupted sternly, "Don't ever use that word."

"What word?" he gasped.

"'Horrid.' That's a sissy word," said his father. "Leave that to your sisters!"

Bill looked aghast at his unsmiling father and realized that he was completely serious. His mother and sisters had stopped talking and were looking at him, puzzled. His father had meant it, but he had meant more. He knew! He suddenly began to cry and pushed back his chair so hard that it tipped over and clattered onto the floor. He bolted upstairs to his room, where he threw himself on the bed.

"How could his father know? How could everyone know?" he gasped out loud between halting sobs. "How could they know already...what I don't even know?" He lay flat, trying to lessen his weight on the heavy winter quilt, to minimize his very being as if he could will his own disappearance, trying in vain to bury his face in the pillow.

THE JURY

I had received my summons to jury duty two weeks earlier, which I carried, creased and grimy from repeated unfolding and folding, in my shirt pocket. It was a form letter with a blurred identification number typed in the left corner, a guarantee of anonymity. With such large numbers of felons or citizens under some form of legal supervision in the District of Columbia, the potential jury pool was small and overworked. But I had never been selected for a final panel. No one wanted a local journalist on a jury, but I got called up frequently for preliminaries nonetheless.

The district court was a large, cement colored building finished with a bland stone facing. Entirely lacking the classical allusions of other government institutions, especially the federal buildings a few blocks away, it was resolutely rectangular in shape, with square windows and a large glass entryway. Although the day was sweltering and humid with the sun, a palpable, hot circle that punctured the opaque blanket of smog, I was pleased I had remembered a jacket because the cold inside was penetrating. Once past the swinging doors of the entrance, there were banks of escalators that crisscrossed up four stories. The marble floors and walls broke up and echoed conversations and amplified the persistent clatter and squeak of high heels. I turned right and walked down the familiar long corridor to the prospective jury room.

Perhaps two hundred people had already assembled in rows of bright, laminated, plastic and aluminum tube chairs. Some were reading newspapers and others novels, and there was an occasional Bible. Others looked inattentively at the large television monitors and the silent action pictured there. Just like the last time, the program was a National Geographic wildlife documentary. I didn't remember if I had ever seen this particular predator show, but I knew the plot: lion cubs born in the spring, the hunt and kill, battle for survival against hyenas and jackals, an attack by a lone, murderous rogue male, poaching for a pride, survival, and then the dawn of another cycle. I often speculated about some deeper, ironic intent behind playing these programs in this place, something that linked them to our forthcoming civic duty. But the metaphors didn't work out. Justice in the District was neither quick, ruthless, nor savage but just boring and as interminable as a winter night in Lapland at the other end of nature's spectrum.

I sat down and glanced around the huge room. Almost no one was talking; no one ever did. Each person appeared to be entirely self-contained and preoccupied, separated into imaginary cubicles of privacy. It was the only crowd I ever encountered where it was impossible to make eye contact with anyone. Even when I tried to fix my glance on the person next to me, she turned away in a gesture, almost the rebuke that I fully expected. I could neither capture nor hold a look. And any accidental exchange instantly dissolved into an unfocused stare. Everyone, it seems, had decided that to attract any attention would doom one to serve on a jury. But I didn't care. I had always wanted to serve but thought I never would. So it was just a matter of waiting out the day.

Jury selection never varied for as long as I could remember. On a central television monitor, numbers would appear periodically, interrupting the predator show, and those whose appeared would then follow a court official to the jury room. I was surprised this time, however, when, after only ten minutes' wait, my number flashed on the screen. I stood and walked with fifty or so others out and down the corridor, up one flight of escalators, down another hallway, and finally into the jury room.

Seated at the front was a judge, wearing his robe, and to his left sat the defendant and his lawyers. Farther on, completing a half-circle around the trial area, sat the district attorney and his assistant. The other half-moon was taken up by the jury box and, next to the judge, the witness box. We were asked to sit down in the orange plush seats of the spectators' section.

Almost immediately, I noticed a bothersome hissing sound, like an amplified leaky valve, an ambient noise purposefully pumped up to drown out confidential discussions between the judge and the lawyers. During the next few days, it would turn on and off at almost regular intervals, obscuring heated discussions about procedure. I could only guess the difficulties (and the winners and losers) from the intensities of hand and arm gestures. The district attorney, who seemed to lose most of these arguments, had the habit of hanging his head in disappointment as he walked slowly back to his chair.

The defendant sat calmly in his chair; he was a very handsome Hispanic or black man around thirty years old. He wore a puffy black-and-white striped sweater and only occasionally glanced to the side to catch the eye of his attorney. Dark-haired with pale, blotchy white skin, she wore a cheap-looking blue suit with a pink scarf around her neck, secured by a large silver clasp. I got the impression that she was very young and probably inexperienced. The district attorney looked ill at ease in his brown suit. He was a tall black man who kept tugging at his shirt cuffs to pull them out from his coat sleeve.

One by one we were called to sit in the jury box. The lawyers and the judge had printouts of our names, addresses, professions, ages, and the brief questionnaires we had filled in. No words were spoken between us, but the lawyers looked over each potential juror carefully. Some were dismissed immediately, and a new person took up the empty chair. I looked carefully and intently at the defendant and then at his lawyer. I guessed that this would either eliminate me quickly or suggest that I might be a good juror. In fact, however, it probably had nothing to do with my fate. The lawyers had their own logic: race, age, and profession calculated as a demographic bet. But I think we all hoped, in one way or another, to affect the choice, which is why almost everyone else looked away, at the ground, or at some invisible focal point over the heads of the lawyers.

Number after number was called, but it became obvious that those of us who remained seated had been chosen. Finally, thirteen numbers were selected—the panel and one substitute. The rest of the group was dismissed back into the waiting room, perhaps to be called up again for another panel.

The judge then turned off the air and looked at us. "Welcome to you, and my congratulations that you have joined us today to fulfill your civic duty. I am Superior Court Justice Andrew Sanders. The defendant's name is Edward Johnson, and his attorney is Ms. Bettina Skolnick. The District of Columbia is represented by James Brown. The charges in the case are first-degree murder. I want to caution you to tell me now if any of you are either related to or acquainted with the defendant in any way." There was silence.

"Johnson," I thought. "Yes, I knew that name. Of course. Johnson was the murderer of the gay minister whom our paper had written about a couple of months ago." It had been a particularly brutal and sensational killing. Johnson was a professional dancer, a stripper, really, and undoubtedly a hustler, who hung out in the warehouse district of the city near the old navy yard. In several of the older buildings adjacent to the bus company pens and fenced-in fields of scrap and junk, there were nightclubs and theaters. On weekend evenings, the entire area was transformed from a deserted, derelict industrial backwater into

THE JURY

Washington's gay and lesbian center. Hundreds of suburbanites flocked to the clubs. It was so busy on Saturday night that the DC police force had to send in officers to direct traffic and parking.

I remembered the story vividly because it was so gruesome. The victim had picked up the hustler somewhere (perhaps there) and taken him back to his house in the city. Very late that night, a housemate—a minister at a local gay congregation—had been awakened by the hustler who needed a key to exit the dead-bolted front door. The hustler claimed the roommate was too drunk to awaken. Only on the afternoon of the next day did the minister discover the roommate's body, his neck grotesquely swollen around a tightly twisted gold-linked chain. There had been no doubt about the identity of the killer. The minister picked him out immediately from mug shots provided by the police.

I was flushed with anticipation. Not only was I on a jury, but it was the jury for a trial that had made headlines in all the local papers. It was more than I might have wanted and probably more than I should do. I thought immediately of telling the judge that I already knew many details of the story; it would probably disqualify me from the jury. But I didn't want to forego the experience. I thought I could find a way to be fair; no one would ever discover what I knew.

I looked around at my fellow jurors, who were staring blankly, perhaps dazed by their misfortune at being chosen. Like any local jury I could imagine, this one presented an unscientific sampling of the city population. There were two large black women, a smartly dressed blond woman who looked something like an executive or a lawyer, a very attractive light-skinned African-American woman, an older man, a pair that looked Latino, a very young white woman, another middle-aged black man, and two other black women, making for totals of five men, seven women, six African-Americans, two Latinos, four whites, and, as far as I could judge, five professionals and seven workers of one sort or another, one of whom might have even been a domestic. This was the sort of mental calculation that each one of us was surely doing simultaneously. It was the silent social ritual that preceded any speech in Washington. The alternative juror, a slender Hispanic man, sat slightly off to the side, emphasizing with his distance his desire not to join us.

The judge looked sternly and reminded us that we were obligated not to discuss the trial with anyone outside the jury deliberation room. The trial, he thought, would probably last three or four days, and for those whose employers
90

would not cover their expenses, there would be a small daily compensation. I pushed back a lingering impulse to mention what I knew about the case.

When the district attorney began his presentation, I wondered if I could stand to listen to him for three days. His voice was pleasant, but his speech was jerky and hesitant, as if he had once memorized the lines but had now forgotten most of them. Searching for the right word, he often came up with a circumlocution or abstraction that made his argument hard to follow. Whether this unnatural rhythm came from nervousness or inexperience or a desire to sound more technical and learned than he was, I thought it would probably alienate almost anyone who tried to catch his argument.

"Mr. Johnson is charged with the crime of murder in the first degree committed with malice with full intention. We will demonstrate that he did enter the victim's house; that they did engage in sexual intercourse; and that afterwards, he did strangle the victim with the murder weapon, a gold chain. Subsequent to this act, he awakened the housemate of the victim and secured exit through the locked and dead-bolted front door.

"The prosecution will present material evidence and witnesses who can corroborate the activities of the victim and the criminal. We will also demonstrate the motive, which in this case was revenge and self-abhorrence, based upon Mr. Johnson's pathological hatred of homosexuals, even though he was one himself and preyed upon them for his livelihood."

As I remembered the case, none of this seemed quite right. Nothing had been said, in our story or research, about a psychological pathology: our reporter had interviewed a police detective who speculated it was just a trick gone wrong and probably a last-minute desire to rob the victim. Johnson had been apprehended with a watch and ring belonging to him. Why bring up this quirky psychological theory of intent to murder? Why not just stick to the facts, unless, of course, the prosecution lacked crucial evidence?

The defense attorney then stood up to summarize her case. Speaking into a microphone, she denied that her client had murdered anyone. Yes, he had been at the house, and yes, he had engaged in intercourse with the victim. But, when he left, he was alive but too drunk to let him out. It had been a surprise and a shock to hear two days later that the man had been murdered in his sleep. As for the evidence—and the attorney drew imaginary quotation marks around the word with her fingers—there wasn't anything that tied her client to a violent act. One could only convict him on a supposition or racial prejudice, not the facts: it was the case of a white man murdered and a black scapegoat, she concluded.

The prosecution called its first witness: a laboratory specialist from the DC Department of Forensics, a dreamy-looking woman with a distant, bored expression on her face. She spoke very precisely and in short bursts of information, as if she had been warned in a hundred prior trials not to embroider or exaggerate her findings. The result was a dreary recital of facts: the cause of death, asphyxiation with a chain the victim wore around his neck; evidence of sexual intercourse; and a room with clothing and books flung around on the floor, although there were no obvious signs of a struggle. She concluded by saying that the house key was lying on the kitchen table in the afternoon when the police had conducted their search.

"Did you find any other relevant evidence?" asked Prosecutor Brown.

"Permission to approach the bench, Your Honor?" the defense attorney interrupted in a clear, abrupt tone—suggesting that she had been waiting for this moment. Both she and Brown walked up to the judge's table, and he turned up the hissing sound. Both lawyers gestured, but I could see that she was winning the point. I took the opportunity to look to my right, into the spectators' section. It was difficult to make out faces because the area was dark while the jury box was lit by several spotlights. I thought there might be ten or so people, perhaps some of them witnesses and perhaps others—friends of the defendant or maybe even the victim's family. The judge nodded as he affirmed his ruling, and the two lawyers returned to their seats.

"I have no further questions," said Brown. I could scarcely believe what I had heard: the evidence of the watch and ring had been suppressed.

The defense attorney stood up behind her desk and looked at her notes. "Detective Blakely," she said, "you said there was no evidence of a struggle? Just evidence of consensual sex?"

"Yes."

"And just where is the gold chain that you say is the murder weapon?"

"Well, we took photographs of the body, and you can see very clearly from these not only the chain but the marks it made in causing the strangulation."

"And just where is that chain now, Officer?"

"Unfortunately, the chain and other evidence have been removed without authorization from the evidence room at police headquarters."

Skolnick leaped to her feet. "Objection, Your Honor," she cried. "There is no other evidence."

"Sustained," affirmed the judge as he glowered at the witness.

Now I understood perfectly what had happened and why the strategy of the prosecution was so bizarre. Somehow the evidence in the case—the gold chain and the incriminating watch and ring—had disappeared. Only the chain could be mentioned because the police had photographed it around the victim's neck.

"Does this happen frequently, to your knowledge, Officer?" asked the defense attorney triumphantly.

"On occasion. Perhaps in ten percent of the cases we handle, evidence is misplaced."

"Or stolen?"

"Or stolen," came the clipped confirmation.

"Or never there in the first place," retorted Skolnick. "That will be all: thank you, Officer," she said as she adjusted the silver clasp on her scarf and sat down.

Brown next called the minister-housemate to testify. He was a small, unpleasant-looking man with very precise gestures and an exasperated expression.

"Are you Samuel Friendly, the victim's housemate?"

"Yes."

"Please tell the jury what you know of this case."

Friendly sat forward in his chair, smoothed his whitish, clipped hair, and began speaking in short, simple sentences. His tone had the trace of a snarl in it, making him sound as if he were either very unhappy or angry—or both—and bothered that he had to testify.

"On the Saturday night of the murder, I went to bed early, probably about eleven. I was very tired, and so I was sound asleep. I didn't hear Jerry come in. Later, the defendant—that man over there," he said, pointing, "woke me up abruptly at around half past two." He said this angrily as if he were still furious about his sleep being interrupted.

"He wanted a key to get out. You see, we always use the dead bolt lock on the front door. It's Washington, DC, after all, and the neighborhood is still in transition. I got up, went downstairs, opened the kitchen drawer where we kept the key, and used it to let him out. Then I went back to bed."

Brown was obviously upset by this choice of words and conscious that his witness was alienating the jury. He got closer to him, as if his presence would soften the answers.

"Why didn't you check on your housemate at that time?"

"Why should I have?" I didn't check with Jerry about every man he brought home. He just lived there. You just don't do that. I only went to look for him after church the next day. He owed me some money for groceries, and I wanted to ask him about it."

"And how did you come to identify Mr. Johnson?"

"Conference, Your Honor, please," broke in the defense counsel. And again the two lawyers conferred with the judge under the irritating fog of noise. This time, however, the prosecutor won because he asked the question again.

With a quick triumphant look at Johnson, Friendly said: "The police showed me several photographs, and I picked his out. There was no doubt."

Now I knew what the conference was about. Johnson obviously had a record. Why else would the police have his photograph—or mug shot? The defense didn't want us to suppose that and surely wouldn't allow any prior convictions to enter the case.

"Mr. Friendly," began the defense counsel, "you said that the defendant woke you up at around half past two on Sunday morning and that he claimed he could not unlock the front door?"

"Yes, that's exactly what I said," he explained with exaggerated patience.

"If so, then why was the key on the front table and not back in the kitchen drawer where you normally kept it?"

"I was very tired and groggy. I think I forgot. It's possible, you know."

"And why was the door unlocked? You made a point of telling us of your fear of the Washington community you lived in. Why not lock the door again?" The defense attorney made a gesture toward straightening her scarf.

"Look," exclaimed the witness. "I was tired; it was late; maybe I made a mistake. Maybe I locked the door; I just don't remember. I made another mistake, too; I should have called the police then and there. Johnson is a murderer!"

"Isn't it because you are lying about what happened, Mr. Friendly? Isn't it entirely consistent with the facts that your housemate told Johnson where to find the key and that Johnson opened the door, put the key on the table, and then let himself out, leaving the door unlocked? After all, how could he lock the door from the outside and still leave the key inside? Isn't that how the real murderer came in? He found an open door, assaulted the victim, and murdered him?" She cut him off abruptly, before he could answer, "Thank you, Mr. Friendly.".

The next witness was a very tall, broad-boned woman with long reddish hair and wearing a heavy brocade skirt. She moved easily and confidently into the chair and prepared herself to answer. Prosecutor Brown rose and approached her.

"For the record, you are Eleanor Gaddis of Washington, DC?"

"Yes," she said.

"Do you know the previous witness, Mr. Friendly?"

"Yes, indeed, he has been an acquaintance ever since I came to Washington in the early eighties. I think I met him at a folk-music concert. We are both active in the local bluegrass movement. I probably see him once or twice a month at various functions and sometimes at church."

Brown looked intently at her as if silently telling her to get to the point.

"What is your impression of the truthfulness of Mr. Friendly, Ms. Gaddis?"

She did not hesitate. "Sam Friendly is one of the most honest and trustful people I know. He would never lie, particularly in a case like this."

Brown looked at the defense. "Your witness."

Skolnick stood up, leaning on her desk with both hands spread in fans around the notes she glanced at.

"You say that Friendly was honest. Did he and the victim get along well? Didn't the victim owe him money for rent and groceries? Weren't they, in fact, not even on speaking terms at this point?"

"Well, I think there was some difficulty over money, yes. But Sam is a very honest person. What he says is the truth. I believe him, entirely," replied Gaddis, almost too emphatically.

The defense attorney looked knowingly at the jury box and sat down.

Brown's last witness was a young, very dramatic black man, perhaps in his mid twenties. Wearing a red, checkered bandanna around his head that clashed with an orange silk shirt, he sat down and crossed his legs with a flourish. Looking around the room at a glance, he ran his eyes across the ceiling as if they were searchlights at a movie opening and then fixed upon the heavy gold ring on his right hand.

"Thank you for coming today, Mr. Duchamps. Please tell us, in your own words, what Mr. Johnson told you about himself—but tell us first how you know him."

Duchamps smiled a stage smile at Brown and then beamed it at us in the jury box. It made me squirm, and I suspected the others reacted in the same way.

"I've known Johnson for two or three years. Our connection is show business. You see, I'm a playwright, and so naturally I was bound to meet up with him sometime. We lead that kind of life: parties, dances, bars, you know. Anyway, I've heard him say frequently how much he hated the life and how he wanted out. Maybe get into show business. He was always talking about it."

"Excuse me," interrupted Brown, "would you explain what you mean by 'the life'?"

"Oh dear, sorry," apologized the witness. He stretched out his right arm, bent his hand stiffly upward, raised his eyebrows, and looked at his ring again. "The gay scene, of course. I think it was too much for him. Anyway, as I was saying, he hated the life, and he particularly hated homosexuals—fags, to use his own words."

"But," broke in Mr. Brown, "he was himself a homosexual."

"Yes and no," replied Duchamps. "Yes, he hired himself out. Yes, he danced at a club. But, no, he hated his life. He often told me that he would kill a fag someday. Exactly those words."

"Let me have confirmation," responded Brown. "Mr. Johnson told you that he would someday murder a homosexual?"

Duchamps put both feet on the floor, leaned forward, and looked at Brown; he paused, looked at the defense attorney, paused again, and then spoke as he turned his head toward us.

"Yes, he said exactly that to me several times."

The cross-examination was such a disaster that I wondered what besides desperation to find a motive had led the prosecutor to put Duchamps on the stand.

"Mr. Duchamps, are you the author of a play called *Cross-Identities*?" began the defense.

"Yes, thank you, I am," beamed the witness.

"I've read the play you wrote," continued Ms. Skolnick. "It's a remarkable piece of fantasy."

"Thank you. Yes, it is a good play. I have several possibilities to put it on. A theater here in town. Something in New York maybe…" Duchamps's voice trailed off as if he had suddenly realized why the question had been asked.

"The main character in this play is named Frank, right? And Frank is a self-hating homosexual, isn't he? Isn't that the point of the play? That Frank can't face himself, so he strikes out at others? Haven't you, in fact, invented both Frank and Mr. Johnson? Johnson is really just a fictitious character to you. Aren't you testifying here today to publicize yourself and your tawdry little drama?"

The last three words hit the witness like three short jabs to the stomach.

"No," he hissed. "It's a great play. I don't lie. Drama doesn't lie."

"I'm through with this witness," said Ms. Skolnick with a look of triumph as she sat down carefully.

The judge glanced at his watch and addressed us and the counsels.

"I understand, Mr. Brown, that this is your last witness. I will therefore adjourn the case until tomorrow morning at ten when we will hear from the defense. And remember, jury members, you are bound to keep silent about anything you have heard at this trial. You may speak to no one about your opinions outside the deliberation room." With that, he turned abruptly and left the room through a doorway cut into the woodwork behind his bench.

The jury filed out together into the hallway where, suddenly, our ties to each other evaporated as if there never had been any bond between this company of strangers. I walked quickly to the escalators and out the front entranceway. Outside, the glare of the sun was sudden and heavy, a heated weight that pressed on every part of my body. The air was acrid with cigarette smoke from the bands of smokers gathered around the doorway and rancid with the smell of thousands of cars beginning their long trips to the suburbs. I spotted a cab and got in.

"Drop me at the *Washington Gazette*. And don't stop to pick anyone else up. I'll pay extra if I have to."

"OK," said the driver in a heavily accented voice. I rolled down the window in spite of the heat. The air in the interior of the cab was sour from a mixture of too many strong smells—perfume, cigarettes, deodorant, dirty upholstery, and an aging, smoking motor that leaked fumes inside.

We reached the building quickly for that time of day, and I paid the cabbie and went inside. In my office, I closed the door and turned on my computer. It squeaked out its electronic melody of greeting and flickered on. I sat down and called up the program that accessed old copies of the *Gazette*. Luckily, articles could be searched for key words. I tried several: *Edward Johnson, homosexual murder*, and *minister and murder*. The last worked, and I clicked through the story.

Most of what I remembered was accurate. The police had arrested Johnson in Washington after his ID. In his possession were a watch and a ring belonging to the victim. Johnson had made no effort to resist, but he was clearly distressed. He had almost no money with him, perhaps because he had been identified so rapidly. The other details of the story were there—the minister's description of being awakened and the history of the key, the dead bolt lock, and, of course, the gold chain murder weapon. There seemed to be no doubt that it was an open-and-shut case.

I sat back in my swivel chair, stretched out my legs, and closed my eyes. "How would I ever deal with all this?" I wondered. It was clear now that the police had bungled the case. Johnson was guilty, and I knew it, so it wasn't a question of objectivity. But how could I tell the other jurors the details I knew? Maybe I could suggest items carefully. But I had no idea if they would accept my story.

The next morning, when I arrived at the courthouse, the sky was the same disheartening smear of orange and green as it had been the day before. I walked quickly into the building and felt released from the folds of moist air outside but still flushed with its heat. In the hallway outside the courtroom, there were benches with several heavyset policemen lounging on them, probably waiting to testify in some of the other courtrooms that opened onto the same area. I walked in and took my place in the almost-full jury box. All the players were there, including the judge and the defendant, who was now wearing a beige shirt and brown tie that showed off his handsome broad shoulders. Ms. Skolnick wore a different suit this time, tailored in a dark shade of blue, with a green neck scarf but the same silver brooch. Mr. Brown had chosen a dark-blue suit. It seemed to fit him better, and his long arms seemed comfortable in it. But I could not understand wearing dark colors in the summertime. It was always a mystery to me that on the hottest days of July during rush hour, a hundred businessmen and -women would jam into the Metro wearing clothes in shades and weights guaranteed to absorb and retain light and heat.

The judge called the court to order. Looking out at the audience, I noticed that it had increased to about twenty. Perhaps someone from my paper was there; I hadn't had time to ask.

"Mr. Brown informs me that he has finished with his case. So now the defense may call its first witness."

Skolnick stood up carefully and walked from behind her desk and into the center of the judicial circle.

"I actually don't have any witnesses, Your Honor. This case has been preposterous from the beginning. I will, in my summation, explain why this charge against Mr. Johnson is entirely unfounded and based upon fabricated and biased evidence. As a consequence, we have no witnesses to call."

She sat down, giving the jury a triumphant look, and folded her hands in front of her. The vaguest hint of distress passed over the judge's face and then vanished.

"If you are prepared to do so now, Ms. Skolnick, you may begin your summation."

"Thank you, Your Honor," she said, rising again. "Yes, we are prepared." Turning to face us, she pushed the papers on her desk to the side but where she still could glance down at what I presumed was a list of points to make.

"This is an accusation and a trial based upon mistakes: mistaken charges, lost and nonexistent evidence, and false presumptions of guilt. My client, Mr. Johnson, is, as was stipulated, a dancer in a local nightclub. You are not being asked to make a judgment about his profession or his private life. It is also true that he went to the victim's home on the evening in question. He admits to having sex with the victim. Then sometime shortly after midnight, he left the premises, waking up the roommate to open the dead bolt lock. We do not know, of course, what happened then. But the only possible explanation is that Mr. Friendly placed the key on the hallway table at the front entrance and left the door open. Sometime during the night, an intruder entered the house through the unlocked door and went upstairs and into the first bedroom on the landing—the victim's. The victim must have awakened, and there was a brief struggle in which he was killed by strangulation. The murderer then searched the room briefly but must have panicked and fled, leaving by the unlocked front door. Who that person might be is a mystery to me and to the DC police, as he surely must also be to you, the members of the jury. This is a case in which my client has been charged with a crime he didn't commit because the police were too incompetent or uninterested to find the real killer. There is a further consideration you might ponder as you deliberate, and that is how the so-called minister, Mr. Friendly, could pick out my client from the photographs shown him. The answer is simple; he had seen him dance at the Gaiety Club in Southeast Washington, where he, too, was a regular customer. As for the fantasies and illusions of Mr. Duchamps, these are best left to some amateur theatre group."

Skolnick looked carefully into the eyes of every juror, one after the other, as she spoke. Her visual gestures seemed, like her brief speech, too rehearsed, as if they came from a textbook about how to influence a jury rather than from any deep conviction. Still, it might be effective on the others. I was amazed, however, that she could concoct such a tale. A defense has to be a defense, of course, but this was clearly a fabrication given what I knew about the case. I didn't think the jurors would fall for it. She had presented no evidence whatsoever of an intruder and had done her best to prejudice us against the prosecution witnesses.

The prosecutor rose, looked at the jury and the judge, and began, glancing from time to time at the defendant.

"I certainly agree that this is a botched, messed-up case. But not because of the police. The fault is the defendant's. Yes, he is a male dancer in a local club, but, as you have heard, he also hated his profession, hated the homosexual underworld that he felt trapped in. We have heard that he found this life intolerable. So, on the night of July 25, 1992, he went home with the victim. They had sex in the bedroom, and then Johnson, either in a rage or with the intent of robbery, strangled the victim.

"Trying to leave quickly, he found that the doors were locked with a dead bolt lock, and he couldn't remember seeing where the victim had placed the key. He must have tried to find it in his pockets and probably looked in a drawer or two. Failing that, he did what he had to do, despite the risk. He awakened the housemate and demanded to be let out. When asked about the victim, he said that he was drunk in his room and couldn't be awakened. Friendly opened the front door, let him out, and then, because he was still only half-awake, closed the door, put the key down on the table, and returned to bed. But there was no intruder; no evidence of any other person has been introduced. The case is very clear. Johnson, in his tortured mind, finally acted on his impulse to kill a homo-

100

sexual—probably he thought he could kill that same tendency within himself. But he only succeeded in murdering an innocent victim."

During his speech, Brown had managed to call up what I thought was genuine anger. But I wondered whether it was anger at the victim, anger at the defense attorney, or—this was most probable—disgust with police forensics for not making a stronger case and for losing crucial evidence that would have convicted Johnson. Or maybe he realized that the motivation he ascribed to Johnson didn't work; perhaps, even as he described it, he recognized he was losing the confidence of the jury.

Judge Sanders cleared his throat, thanked the two attorneys, and then sent us to the jury deliberation room, making sure to warn us not to discuss the case with anyone outside of the jury and instructing us to select a foreperson to lead discussion and record votes.

The jury deliberation room was shabby and windowless, a sealed envelope of stale, bureaucratic air. There was a large Formica table with two stacks of notebooks and a box of pencils, several plastic chairs, and an uncomfortably close adjacent bathroom. We entered and, not yet sitting, moved around the table, as if exercising a last resistance to being there. Gradually, everyone found a place and sat down.

I looked around the room at my fellow jurors with a sense of excited uneasiness. The elegant young black woman cleared her throat and said, "I think, first, we need to elect a foreman. Has anyone here ever served on a jury? Been a foreman?" There were a few mumbled responses. Several people looked away or down at the table. "Well, I have," she continued. "Perhaps I should do it again. It will save time."

I wondered at her insistence, perhaps because I wanted to be the foreman myself. Perhaps that way I could steer the jury to a decision they would have to make on botched evidence. But I couldn't bring myself to object. If I appeared too eager, I might be suspect. Better to wait to convince the others later. So, we all agreed.

"Excellent," she began. "First, everyone should take a half sheet of paper and write his or her first name on it. Fold it and put it in front of you so we can address one another easily." For the next minute or two, there were sounds of tearing paper and the scarcely audible scratching of pencils. Everyone wrote their names and then folded the papers into tents so they would stand up in front of them. I glanced around at the other eleven and stopped, amazed, at the sheet in front of the older white man. He was glowering but at no one in particular. Instead of a first name, he had written his juror's number on the sheet. I couldn't contain myself.

"What's the matter?" I asked. "Why don't you write your name like everyone else?"

"Just my number," he said remotely. "That's all you're getting." He must have believed that in doing this he could avoid talking or responding to questions or participating at all. It was as if he had stepped outside the room. The other jurors looked disconcerted, and I suspected several were jealous of his ploy. By giving their first names they had acknowledged being a part of the group and its unpleasant task.

During the next hour or so, we examined the evidence that the court had accepted: several photographs of the victim, his neck grotesquely swollen around the gold chain, a disorderly bedroom, and the mug shots from which Friendly had identified the defendant. I tried to guess what each juror thought as he or she handled the material. Some were very hesitant to pick up the photographs; others stared at them as if trying to read a difficult passage in a language they understood badly; some quickly passed them on. No one said a word.

The foreperson—her name was Evelyn, as I now knew—cleared her throat and began again. "Before we discuss the evidence, I think we should have a straw poll to see where we all stand. Then we can talk about doubts, issues, and so forth. I suggest we vote three ways: not guilty, not sure, guilty." She reached for a pad, ripped off six sheets, tore them in two, and quickly passed them around. I was impressed with her abrupt efficiency and noted the order in which she placed our choices.

We passed our folded ballots around to her, and she opened each of them, pressing back the fold with the heel of her hand and recording the vote on her pad.

"Nine not guilty; one not sure; two guilty." she reported. "So, now, let's see why three of you think that Mr. Johnson might have committed this crime."

I couldn't believe what I had heard. Nine not guilty when he had so clearly done it. Why had they voted like that? Probably, I thought, because of the preposterous motivation invented by the prosecutor to cover up the incompetence of his office. Unless, of course, the prosecutor really believed it, in which case it was just a terrible miscalculation. But how could I convince the others to come to an opinion that I had only arrived at because of the story in my newspaper? If

I told them what I knew, I would probably be removed from the jury, in which case there would be no chance of conviction. If I didn't tell them, what could I say?

"I'd like to say a few things," I ventured. "First, I think that the prosecution is wrong about the motivation in this case. I'm not even sure this is first-degree murder because that depends upon intent. It's possible there was some sort of struggle, something that went wrong. So I would be willing to opt for second-degree murder. I think Johnson was probably trying to rob the victim and killed him—perhaps even accidentally. But that's a better explanation. Furthermore, it's not really possible for anyone else to have committed the murder. There was no one else in the house at the time."

"What about the minister?" shot back the foreperson.

"This whole thing disgusts me…a minister at that," interjected the heavy-set black woman who had identified herself as Ida.

"So what?" I said to her incautiously. "And it's crazy to think that the housemate would do it."

"First, I'm not crazy," replied the foreperson. "And second, it's Mr. Johnson. Please have some respect for the people you are talking about," she cautioned me, "even if you presume their guilt."

As if she had not heard this brief interruption, Ida continued: "I don't even think that poor boy was murdered at all. How can we be sure?"

"Well, if he wasn't murdered, how did he die?" I asked impatiently.

"Fell and hit his head on the corner of the bed."

I couldn't believe what I was hearing. The photographs of the room had clearly shown that the bed was just a mattress on some sort of supporting frame with no extruding edges. But worse, I could feel the animosity gathering in the room. What was it? It couldn't be racial, because number 2043 sat and glowered at me as belligerently as the foreperson.

"I'm certain that the motivation was robbery," I began again. "Mr. Johnson may not have intended to kill Jerry, but he certainly did. Who else could have gotten in? The defense offered no witnesses, nothing to prove there was a fourth person who entered the house that night."

"What makes you so certain that it was robbery? How can you know for sure? Nothing seems to have been missing. I think that Evelyn is right. The prosecution hasn't proven anything. There's no evidence to convict Mr. Johnson. I think I'll change my vote." This was said carefully by one of the Latino women.

I looked around the room for a friendly or encouraging face, but no one responded. I realized that I was quickly losing them all. The only way to convict Johnson was to reveal what I shouldn't have known. Perhaps if I explained to them about the newspaper story, they would understand. But more probably, they would think I was lying. And I couldn't trust Evelyn not to go straight to the judge to report me.

"Well," I said, "I'll concede about first-degree murder, but I'll never change my vote on second-degree. If I have to hang up this jury for a week, I'll do it."

"So, you have some sort of special knowledge about this case that's a mystery to all of us," urged Evelyn sarcastically, "and you intend to keep us here until we agree with you?" She said this while looking around the room and gathering up a majority of hostile glances.

"Yes," I said almost desperately, "I won't give in. And, no, I have no more secrets than the rest of you do."

TOO CLOSE

He felt a mounting and familiar uneasiness. The temptation of loneliness was to give in completely to it, to immerse oneself in doing small things and marking the welcome speed of the hours as they passed into the next day. There had been many days or, rather, many evenings like this of late. He had not expected the relationship to last very long—they somehow never did—and that had always been the implicit understanding. They had discussed this in large, abstract terms, usually when speaking of friends, but never touching the specifics of their own future together. Sometimes it was joking; sometimes playful; sometimes regretful; but he and Stephen had always recognized the impermanence. When they went to a restaurant and saw other couples, paired ostentatiously, they always laughed: "They think it will last, but who are they kidding?" "Themselves," was always the quick answer, said knowingly as if the two of them were the only ones brave enough or clearheaded enough to see the impossibility of a lasting future together. There were some long-term couples he knew, but it was impossible to imagine what dynamic kept them together. Certainly, it had to be habit more than anything else, something strangely like a shared loneliness and the two of them engaged in doing small things and marking off the time.

He realized that his thinking had become too cynical. Stephen had taken a job in California, something he had always dreamed of doing, and, for a while, there were coast-to-coast trips and long phone calls and daily e-mails. But these had trailed off, diminished by distance and inattention, until both of them realized the futility of keeping on with it. They both understood that the very freedom and mobility that had made their relationship possible and momentarily acceptable had also rendered it fragile. How many straight couples had become like them, he wondered? Whoever said that social trends began at the edge of society and then became the middle-class norm was right. But to be a pioneer of diminished commitment was no comfort even if others would eventually suffer the same fate...

TOO CLOSE

He recognized that all of these thoughts were rationalizations for the inertia he felt. Something like this train of thought eventually stirred him to break through his lethargy, as if it took philosophy to drive him from his apartment. Well, he would try; he would go out anyway.

Since it was a very hot and muggy night in Washington, he decided to dress lightly—a pair of black pants and a striped, button-down shirt he had bought in Paris. He also decided to shave again and scrub his face to soften the shiny glaze that the heat and humidity of the day had left on his skin. He was careful not to study his face too closely in the mirror. It was easier to reassure himself: "Fifty wasn't a bad age, after all." And regular late afternoons at the gym had given him a slightly square, athletic look. He regretted the expanding bald spot in front and often wore a cap to cover it. Many of his friends had made insincere comments about him: "Bald men are really sexy," and "It's a sign of sexual energy." But to reduce aging to such sad clichés that no one really believed was hardly a comfort and, in his experience, false anyway.

The walk to Seventeenth Street was a short one from his apartment, but this evening, in particular, it seemed tedious. Even at midnight, the thick, heavy air still held the day's heat like a gauze curtain over the city. Moving through the moist atmosphere felt vaguely like stepping through a silky cobweb strung out along the street. He brushed at his skin occasionally to find nothing there but the vague impression of substance.

The town houses along the sidewalk were immaculately painted and carefully tended. Each entrance was distinct, sometimes with cast-iron steps and railings and usually with a heavy front door with a high window revealing the ceiling of the closed entrance hallway. Others had an English basement apartment that opened under the main entrance. A few houses had a typical Washington curved bay window (an impossible interior space to furnish) while others were flat and worked out with intricate brick patterns. House fronts, he often speculated, spoke a language of very limited vocabulary, mixing and matching the few available motifs in a style that was both elegant but always cramped. It was surprising how small and dark these nineteenth-century town houses were, with their interior divisions, doors, and high archways. Some of his friends had gutted the interiors, clearing out obstacles and opening up spaces with the ingenious placement of kitchen cabinets, elaborate and elegant workplaces, and built-in eating coves. The mechanics of living that the nineteenth century had sought to hide and repress—its tiny cramped kitchens and its hidden bathrooms—had been opened up for all to see and admire. These new public places proclaimed themselves in gleaming Italian marble, expensive, richly grained wood, and white plastic celebrated by the touch of a flamboyant bouquet of flowers. But on such a night, he thought, they were more like air-conditioned mausoleums, like old men standing in a row begging for a youthful knock at the door.

He reminded himself not to be gloomy.

The streets were still busy with cars nosing along slowly looking for places to park and couples and individuals walking purposefully or simply sauntering along, chatting and laughing. Occasionally, a man walked alone (as he did) eyeing other men, searching their faces for welcoming signals, but careful, at the same time, not to look too long at the blank, unresponsive faces of rejection. He walked along, watching but not playing the game.

At the corner of Seventeenth and R Streets, he turned left and continued. The street was jammed with strollers, small knots of friends talking animatedly, and others, like himself, intent upon destinations. On warm nights like this, restaurants spilled out onto the broad sidewalk, and the whole street was filled with the dim chimes of clinking glasses and plates and muffled crashes of laughter. Most of the crowd was quite young, in their twenties or early thirties, and dressed casually but carefully in jeans, white T-shirts, and sneakers. "Why," he wondered, "did living at the fringes of society, breaking its cardinal rules, lead to such conformity?" Putting the question this way seemed to answer itself, for the stresses of living secret, furtive, or at least disapproved lives was often the only radicalism that they could manage. In every other way, so many of the men he knew were conservative, even rock-ribbed Republicans.

He quickly reached the entrance to the bar, pulled open the door, and climbed the staircase into a din of voices. There was no discernible reason for the name of the establishment: The Harbor. It might have been chosen to remind patrons of sailors, or perhaps it was an establishment that had moved from some other location where the name made more sense. This was probably the reason; gay bars often migrated, following along as fashions and neighborhoods shifted. The same indifferent wind that blew relationships together and then apart also scattered the businesses that catered to gay life.

The room he entered was large, long, and dimly lit in soft reds and yellows. A long mirrored bar ran along half of the length with stools scattered in front. Against the opposing wall stood more stools and several high pedestal tables. The far end of the room had several dark armchairs stationed in front of a tiny, unused dance floor. The absence of loud music indicated an older crowd. Despite an obvious breeze of air-conditioning, the atmosphere was acrid with smoke. The crowd was thick, particularly around the bar, and he recognized a number of regulars. At least half of the patrons stood alone, their eyes sweeping the room discreetly, always returning to the entrance as if expecting a friend. It amazed him that so many men who came alone and would leave alone could look so preoccupied, could give the impression of waiting for someone late to an appointment. It was an acquired skill: to be alone and hungry and not look it.

He interrupted the young bartender's conversation and ordered a beer. The cold, glistening bottle was refreshing in his hand, although he knew that the chilled liquid would quickly become flat and tasteless as he sipped it. He climbed onto the only available stool and nodded noncommittally to the man sitting next to him. In his repertoire of greetings, this was the briefest and least of all. It involved no change of expression: eyes were focused elsewhere, and there was no movement of the lips. He preferred it to the more ambiguous salute with a bottle or a glass, which could mean almost anything and was easy to misinterpret.

He looked tentatively around the room, returning to the fixed point of the entranceway. To pass the time, he scored the entrance of each man or couple. The highest marks he gave to those who managed to cause a slight flurry of attention, attracting glances for a moment by some graceful movement or an odd juxtaposition of clothing or generating their own spotlight of beauty and youth. At the low end of such arrivals was the man who paused before entering and then moved quickly to the center of the room and looked up as if to convey the impression that he had been there for hours. The middle grade went to the energetic man who burst in, purposely making a noise with a laugh or some exaggerated movement and then looking around to catch the eyes of anyone who noticed. This was not a game, he knew, that would amuse him for very long.

He put his beer bottle on the bar and, with a damp paper napkin, rubbed his eyes, which were beginning to smart from the cigarette smoke. As he did so, he heard a voice on his left say, "Do you mind if I put my drink here?" "Sure," he said, not looking up and moving his stool slightly to accommodate the stranger. He put the napkin away, seized the bottle in his right hand, and turned slightly to see the man standing next to him. He only responded because the voice had a soft lilt, an accent that clearly belonged in the British family, although to what branch he was not sure.

The man wore dark pants and a white shirt with rolled sleeves. In the rich, somber, smoky atmosphere, his skin still had a pale, shiny patina. He was slight and somewhat shorter than himself, with blondish hair that had begun to evacuate his forehead, leaving only straggling tufts as a kind of rear guard to belie an advancing baldness. He wore heavy but fashionable glasses.

"I can't quite place the accent," he said. "Sounds like English but with a faraway quality."

"Very far away, indeed!" laughed the man.

He thought then that he recognized the pinched syllables of Australian.

"Australia, then?"

"No, even further along: New Zealand. My name is Alan Worthing."

"Bill," he said, carefully following the rule of giving up only his first name, even though Alan had volunteered more. He wasn't sure if he should offer to shake hands. Often, he thought, the British friends he knew shied away from a casual touch, even the gay friends. But for some reason, he reached out, and Alan seized his hand.

"You must be visiting Washington," he remarked, turning on the stool to face Alan completely. "We always apologize for the weather here. It's much too hot and steamy in the summer. The British once even considered this a tropical posting and authorized diplomats to wear shorts on formal occasions. Not pith helmets, of course. And winter, well…" he let his voice trail off as if the season were unworthy of elaboration.

"Oh, I've been here several times," Alan exclaimed. "And it's hardly a hardship. I actually like Washington."

"So why did you come to The Harbor?" Bill interrupted. "It's not one of the flashier bars on the strip. In fact, it's rather staid." He stopped, recognizing that he had begun by apologizing for the weather and now for the bar and perhaps for himself. It was the classic progression of small talk that might or might not lead to something more interesting, when one of them decided to venture a personal thought or volunteer a portion of his identity.

"It's recommended in the gay guide to the United States that I bought."

"I'm curious," he said. "What was the description?"

"Something like this: 'Conservative but friendly. Generally an older crowd.'"

"And is it?" Bill interjected.

"The friendly part is certainly true," replied Alan warmly. "Do you live in Washington? I assume you're not a tourist like me—that would be too much; two strangers brought together by a gay guide. That's not so much star-crossed as an accident of shopping."

"Yes, I'm a native insofar as anyone really lives in this place. I've been here about twenty years or so. It's curious. I've heard many people admit to living in Washington, but no one is really from here. There isn't any soil for roots to take hold. Everyone has somewhere else that they hail from. I came here to teach at one of the local universities and ended up mired in tenure. You know: in academics, once you have a permanent job, it becomes almost impossible to move!"

"I'm just the opposite," Alan offered. "I'm in the diplomatic corps, which means that nothing is ever permanent except the anticipation of some upcoming posting. So far I've been primarily to English-speaking assignments, although I suppose anything is possible."

"So, are you the ambassador from New Zealand?" Bill laughed.

"Oh, no, at least not yet. It's a civil service appointment, and you can work your way up, presumably to become an ambassador. We don't make these political appointments like you do."

"So you could be an ambassador someday. But as for no politics, I don't really believe you. A civil service without sharp knives doesn't exist. Where are you posted now?"

"All right," Alan smiled. "But just now I'm between positions."

"So," Bill exclaimed, "a redundant diplomat! How long is your visit to Washington?"

"I've been here three days, and I'm to be in New York tomorrow night to meet with the UN delegation."

They had suddenly reached that moment in such encounters where there are several choices. It could end with a quick handshake and departure with a few mumbled words—"Nice to talk to you," or "Well, enjoy the rest of your stay." He might offer the names of a few of his favorite restaurants. Or they could pick up the level of the conversation. They hadn't mentioned politics yet, and, surely, Alan was up on everything happening in the city. Bill wasn't sure what he wanted, so he let Alan break the silence.

"Look, I apologize for being so forthright, but I am here just this last night. Would you like to come back to my hotel with me?"

He looked at Alan seriously now—actually, for the first time—to see if he felt any physical symptom of desire.

"Where are you staying?" he asked, postponing a reply.

"Downtown, somewhat close to the embassy. We could take a cab. It's a very short ride."

"Why not come to my place?" Bill offered. "We can walk...just a few blocks."

Climbing down from his stool, he wondered why he had agreed despite having no discernible reason to or enthusiasm about it. The only relationships that meant anything, he knew from experience, began in desire and then blossomed into friendship. But with Alan, he thought he had found someone he might like as a friend. As for anything else, well, perhaps, but things were, in his rulebook, starting off all wrong.

They pushed through the curtain of thick, damp air that hung around the entrance and out onto the street and then strolled back toward Bill's apartment. Given that Alan was a visitor to Washington, Bill chatted about the city and the buildings they passed, but after four blocks he had pretty much exhausted all the tourist small talk he knew: restaurants, bars, museums, and parts of the city he liked, like Dupont Circle, and parts he avoided, like Georgetown. He was about to plunge into the second layer of chat about local politics and his jokes about being among the few Americans without the right to vote when Alan stopped him, lightly touching his arm.

"You do go on, don't you?" he laughed.

"Yes, it's the insider's tour of the city in ten minutes. Guaranteed to keep you from making any mistakes: don't turn right when you should go left." Bill found Alan's curt attitude a pleasure.

They reached the apartment building in another half block. Bill unlocked the glass front door, and they stepped into the dazzling glare of the foyer.

"Sorry about this," Bill explained. "Someone thinks that glamour and class are measured in kilowatts. It's not quite so awful in the daytime."

"Does that mean I'm spending the night?"

"We'll see," Bill replied, lightly steering Alan into the elevator.

When they entered the apartment, Bill was glad that he had given the room an attentive eye before he left. Of course, his desk was still a mess—there was no way to keep order when he was writing something—but the dishes were done and the bed made. He had not arranged any of his books, and, on the coffee table, there was a John Grisham novel he had just finished after an airplane trip. (He had vowed afterward to never read another.) And there was a contemporary novel he was deciding whether to continue reading and a new edition of Fitzgerald stories he was supposed to review.

Alan followed his glance to the coffee table and reached down to touch the novel with his finger.

"I know the writer," Allan said. "I met him once at a cultural event in New York. A nice enough person, but the writing lacks energy." And, interrupting himself, he asked, "What do you do?"

Out of cautious habit, Bill gave him half an answer. "I teach American literature at a university."

"Does this place have a name, or is it only fictional?" Alan said, looking at him curiously. "You open your apartment to me; you invite me in; you plan to seduce me; but you won't tell me the name of your university?"

"I'm not sure who is doing what to whom quite yet," Bill replied. "But, sure, George Washington University, between here and Georgetown. In the English Department."

"And you have a last name, too?" Alan shot back, pushing his advantage.

"Yes: Johnson."

This could continue a long time, the blunt questioning followed by literal answers in which he volunteered no more than was asked. It was part of the game he had played a hundred times before, because none of this information was necessary, not yet. And to ask such questions, to know more about someone, implied some sort of emotional commitment. Bill fiddled with the top button of his shirt, which he always did when he was nervous.

"Well, telling you my name isn't exactly a proposal of marriage I guess. Speaking of which," Bill continued, "you're married, aren't you?"

"Yes," Alan replied. "How did you know?"

"I didn't. But all this is against my better judgment," Bill said quickly. "Or perhaps just my fate. Do you want something to drink? A beer? Some water?"

"No, I'm fine," said Alan quietly, as if to end the small talk.

Bill understood and reached out to clutch Alan's arm. He guided him into the bedroom, where they quickly undressed, Alan carefully folding his clothing and Bill just stepping out of his apparel, letting it fall to the floor.

"Lights on or off?" asked Bill.

"Stop talking and come to bed," said Alan. Bill turned out the light, pulled down the bedcovers, and wrapped his arms around Alan's shoulders, feeling his slightly moist skin and smell. Now he felt the desire he had been waiting for... the body's always surprising gift to itself.

The next morning was a rushed affair. Alan had a meeting at ten and needed to stop by his hotel first. During coffee, which Bill made very strong and sweet with boiled milk, Alan looked intently into his cup as he held it below his chin.

"Can you see your reflection? Or are you dreaming?" asked Bill.

"Dreaming."

"Of me?"

"No—yes, last night."

"So now I've become something insubstantial, some image from the past you can conjure up when you're with your wife," Bill said sharply.

"That was unkind, but, no, my wife and I have almost nothing to do with each other. It's been that way for years. I got married in the midst of a passion that just as suddenly disappeared. Can you understand that? It happens. But I found myself with a daughter and a career before I knew it."

"How old is she?" Bill asked. "Not your wife."

"About twelve."

"And so now you'll return to all that, right?" Bill said, making the question sound like an accusation.

Alan put his coffee cup down on the table and looked squarely at Bill.

"I have to be in New York at the UN again next month for a meeting with the ambassador. Come up and spend the weekend with me."

"That sounds more like an order than an invitation. I could probably make it. But what about your wife and daughter? Don't they come with you ever?"

"Not this time. Meet me," Alan repeated.

"I'll let you know. I've written my name and phone number on a card. Be in touch." With this, Bill passed the paper across the table. Alan picked it up, his eyes pausing on Bill's last name as if checking that it was still the same, and then slipped it into his shirt pocket.

They stood up together, as if responding to the same cue. Conversations like this travelled in a remarkably narrow gauge. When two people had shared intense intimacy but hardly knew each other, there was a limited vocabulary of gestures, expressions, words, and silences that they could share between them. They both walked toward the door of the apartment, Alan leading. When they reached it, he turned around and suddenly embraced Bill, holding him tightly. Bill experienced a wave of emotion that he quickly repressed with a laugh.

"You'd better go now. Be in touch."

"Yes," said Alan as he slipped outside.

Billed gazed at the closed door, turned around, and began to assess the damage. He had ignored a principle based on long experience: never get involved with a married man. It was a rule he often broke, always to his regret, because the ending was the same. He could never persuade the other person to see that his own risk was just as great: that the pain and anguish of falling in love and risking rejection was as great as betraying any of the responsibilities that marriage brought. Life was more than duty, he often said, but it was an unconvincing argument in the face of the bonds that society imposed on people. Marriage was an institution, above all, and its inmates, he often joked, were free to leave but chose incarceration anyway. At the same time, he knew that these arguments were just that—arguments—and they were unequal to the task of motivating anyone to act. They were plausible only in the aftermath, as an explanation for what had already happened. And, in a way, they increased the hurt, for, knowing that change was possible, that another life could be opened up, that a chance could be seized and lived, made the inevitable end of the affair a painful banality. He would not, he promised, go to New York or let Alan become anything more than a onetime self-deception.

For three days, he heard nothing from Alan and assumed—or, better, rationalized—that the banter about staying in touch meant nothing and the trip to New York was off. That was just as well, he told himself. It would save the trouble of telling Alan that he could not come after all and being unable to give a reason except that he'd had a change of plans. But then, on the fourth night, at about eight, the phone rang. For some reason, Bill was certain that it was Alan.

"Where in the world are you? New York?" said Bill.

"Oh, no. Back in Wellington," replied Alan. "Sitting at the bottom of my garden on a cell phone."

"That means it must be daytime, unless you're a sleepwalker. What time is it? What day is it?"

"One o'clock in the afternoon and tomorrow. We Asians are a step ahead of you."

"And does the sun really shine from the wrong part of the sky?" Bill asked.

"Only from your perspective. North to us means summer and warmth. And that's where you are. Is this a good time to call?"

"Yes," said Bill, surprised at the suggestion that there might be more calls from halfway around the world. "I'm generally back from the gym or shopping, usually eating dinner about now. Weekends are less good at this time…at least, I hope."

"I'm still coming back to New York in two weeks. I'll give you the hotel name when I know it. You'll meet me, won't you?"

"Still giving orders, are you? Yes," said Bill automatically, "I'll be there."

Over the next two weeks there were calls almost every night and two long, chatty letters. They never discussed anything about themselves, but Bill could feel himself slipping gradually into feeling comfortable, confident, and even trusting. It was not what he wanted or expected of himself. At best, any long-distance relationship would be occasional and staccato, with short trips, intense days and nights, and then long periods when the affair would languish. And he could readily predict the ending, yet he could also feel himself entering the Planning Stage (as he sarcastically named it), a dangerous time when he began to think of future meetings, of possible conversations, and to hope for something meaningful. Perhaps, he reasoned, this would work out. This might be enough.

He stepped expectantly into the hotel lobby and looked for Alan, who he thought would be waiting for him as they had planned. But there were no familiar faces, and so he walked over to the desk to call the room. After five rings, the call bounced back to the desk, and the clerk asked if Bill wanted to leave a message.

"No, no message. I'll wait." He turned and walked slowly to the slightly elevated area with large armchairs and sofas in plain view of the front entrance. Luckily, he had brought a novel with him on the train, the newest venture of a woman writer he knew. About a doomed relationship, it had been a disappointment from the beginning. Something about the writing put him off. Was it hurried? Mechanical? Inevitable? Describing something too much like his own predicament? He read several pages but glanced up frequently, feeling a vague, mounting anxiety. He knew he could never turn his own life into a novel. He

could never fix his attention long enough not to look up expectantly for seren-
dipity to change everything, to break into the inevitable logic of fiction.

He waited for over an hour, confident that Alan would appear but, at the
same time, growing angry at his lack of consideration. There had been so many
words casually expended in letters and calls when none at all were required and
now, suddenly, a silence fraught with unpleasant possibilities and inadequate
excuses. Bill wondered if their relationship had already skipped to the phase of
Missed Appointments. "But the calls and letters," he reassured himself. Looking
down at the open novel in his lap, he planned the next minutes carefully. "I'll
read ten more pages to the end of the chapter. If he's not here by then, I'll leave
a message and have a drink." Stretching and measuring time like this was the
best way to control his disappointment.

His eyes fell back onto the page, and as he began to read again, he heard
Alan's voice.

"Really sorry to be late. No excuses right now. How are you, Bill?"

Bill looked up. "You're wearing your diplomat's uniform, aren't you?
Dark suit, somber tie, white shirt, tie. You've exchanged mystery for imper-
sonality."

"Come up to my room," replied Alan, smiling. "I'll change, and we can
have dinner."

Bill stood up and hugged Alan, letting his lips brush against Alan's cheek.

"OK," he said. "Lead the way."

The next two days were filled with visits to museums, long conversations,
dinners, and time spent in the hotel room. Bill was amazed at the natural flow
of their talk and their comfortable physical intimacy. Everything about the time
seemed natural, almost inevitable. Even New York, a city he sometimes detest-
ed for its arrogance and hostility, became a friendly backdrop for their dialogue.
Bill felt as if he were a character in a play reading poetry that only someone else
could have written. These were not his feelings or even his own words; they
came from a place that he reasoned could not be inside him, could not be of his
authorship. He did not want to say words like these; it meant losing control of
reticence, fear, and experience and inviting disaster.

Two hours before his train and Alan's cab back to the airport arrived, they
sat in the lobby.

"I should tell you something important now," said Alan.

"It has to do with your being late that first day, doesn't it?" replied Bill quickly. "I've wondered about your refusal to make excuses."

"The excuse is a rather large one," Alan interrupted. "I was meeting with the ambassador. That's why I was late. In point of fact, I've been promoted. I'm to be second at the embassy."

"Which embassy? I thought you worked in New Zealand," Bill shot back.

"Our service isn't really like yours. We are all civil servants, and we can be posted anywhere for three years or so."

"And you could eventually become an ambassador? Only one step left."

"I suppose so, yes," Alan replied.

"So, where is this mysterious posting on your climb to the top?" Bill chuckled.

"Washington. I'm to be there in one month."

"With your wife and daughter?"

"Yes."

Bill reached over to touch Alan's shoulder and gripped it firmly.

"That's wonderful. We can see much more of each other now. Great!"

Alan looked troubled, even furtive. "I don't know about that."

"But, Alan, you said your marriage was meaningless. And you can surely steal time from your job. It can't be that overwhelming."

"I don't know," said Alan, looking away.

"Damn you!" Bill exclaimed ferociously. "Doesn't this weekend mean anything at all to you? And your calls all the way from New Zealand? What was that about? What are you saying?"

Alan turned and looked at him darkly, and Bill realized that he had seen every emotion on his face before but this one. "It has meant everything to me. I'll never forget. But I can't see you again in Washington. My wife, my job, my daughter. How can I explain?"

"I can explain," cried Bill. "It's cowardice!"

"Not at all. Rather more like duty. I have obligations to all sorts of people. I can't change that. And it wouldn't be right for you or me. You need to get on with your life."

"But this is my life," Bill replied, realizing suddenly that he was making up a flimsy argument and that Alan had already made up his mind. He couldn't stop himself, however.

"Did you plan this as a last fling, then?"

"Don't be cruel. Of course not. Nothing was settled for sure until I saw the ambassador. I've meant everything I've said and done. It's just too much for me."

"So," retorted Bill. "I understand. If you were posted to Great Britain or France, we could meet on the Riviera or in Italy for a week. But you couldn't travel from the embassy to my apartment in Dupont Circle."

"Yes, something like that. You see, I'm bringing too much baggage with me, and you need to understand that," replied Alan sadly.

Bill saw the grief on his face but refused to acknowledge it.

"No, of course I don't understand you. I never will. You're afraid of life, of emotion, of opening up."

"But it is life I'm talking about. Mine…the people who depend upon me, my daughter."

"I won't wait for you," said Bill. "That's completely out of the question."

"I don't expect that; don't want you to. Just keep this weekend as a wonderful memory."

"Memory isn't life," replied Bill. "For me, it just serves as a lesson learned, a caution, or whatever you want to make of it, however you manipulate it. But it's never life."

Alan was silent for a minute. "I have to go. I'm sorry…and I'm happy, too. It was a fantastic time."

He stood up, put the back of his hand on the side of Bill's face, turned, and then picked up his suitcase. He walked slowly out of the hotel and downstairs to the lineup of waiting yellow taxis.

Bill sat motionless. "Yes," he said to himself. He knew exactly what Alan meant and that both elements of his contradiction were completely true and honestly felt. He also knew that he had let himself go; he had broken every rule he'd built up from experience. He stood up and grabbed his small bag. His mind began to race ahead. There was laundry and shopping to do, lectures to write, and the gym to visit when he got home. He might even have the time and courage to finish the sketch for his novel on the train.

ENDING UP IN FLORIDA

Bill walked quickly, despite the heavy carry-on bag he lugged behind him. The terminal he entered at National Airport was the original building, its 1930s-style square modernism now made lopsided with nondescript glass additions and a long, curved, covered walkway for discharging and picking up passengers. The boxy interior was empty except for a crowd clumped around the Esprit Airlines check-in counter. He thought, as he frequently did now, about much-earlier days of flying, without the crowds and security and when airlines served food—in fact, when airlines actually served. But he had had no choice. This was the only flight he could find to Fort Lauderdale on short notice—a sure sign of his reluctance to plan ahead. Inevitably, he would share it with two hundred college students on spring break and the odds and ends of permanent residents returning home. Some of the students came already dressed down for the vacation in shorts, sweatshirts picturing the mascots of local universities, plastic flip-flops, and halter tops; there were a few muscle shirts. Bright-eyed but anxious to be having a good time and self-conscious of their youth, they shuffled in a confused, rambling queue toward the counter.

When his turn finally came, he set the printout of his reservation on the counter and handed the unsmiling attendant his credit card as an ID. She took it and, without comment, passed him his boarding pass.

"Next time, sir," she warned, "use the automatic check-in machine, or there will be an extra charge. And I would earnestly advise you, since this is a two-hour trip, to use the bathroom before you get on the plane. Here," she added in a confidential tone, pulling out a bilious-colored sheet, "is a list of drinks you should probably avoid an hour before take-off: common diuretics." She handed him the paper that had *coffee* written in red warning letters across the top, followed by *tea* and a list of various colas and juices.

"We make sure that all of our elderly customers are fully informed."

He grabbed the paper and stuffed it into his jacket, passed through security, and waited to board. Once inside the plane and with his bag stowed, he relaxed, snapped on his seat belt, and began to contemplate the trip. It was risky business—foolish, even—but he had never shied from taking chances, particularly with relationships, and he felt confident that he could make a choice between Fort Lauderdale and Sarasota and between two friends who had each offered to put him up. Whether these friendships would bloom into something lasting, even beautiful, he had no idea. That was part of his mission: to decide if he could retire to Florida and perhaps with Todd or Mort. Or neither one, if it didn't work out. But the possibilities excited him. He had always prized an open-ended way of life and adventures that began at the end of the runway. It seemed that all of the best the best moments of his life had begun by picking up luggage from a carousel somewhere: Nice, Istanbul, Sydney, Berlin. Even now that he was older and poised on the edge of a final commitment, he felt the same thrill of stepping rather innocently into a surprise scenario that he could only imagine. Except that this time, he felt a strong compulsion to choose, to make a lasting commitment that would also be like an ending.

His reverie was interrupted by the voice of a flight attendant distorted slightly by the loud speaker, although he could see no one. She advised passengers of the usual safety regulations and procedures and then described the mechanics of purchasing drinks and food items. Using the small touch screen computer on the face of the seat back, she explained, one could select from possible offerings, from water to a Caesar salad with various toppings. "Leather in three colors and textures," he mumbled, trying to keep his good humor. Once paid by credit card, the item would be distributed from the automated food cart.

He looked up in disbelief at this last detail, giving the young woman sitting next to him a knowing smile, an invitation to share the absurdity with her. But she was fully absorbed in sending a text message, her thumbs jumping nimbly across her phone keypad as they tapped out the letters. As the plane roared into the air, he nudged her gently with his elbow.

"Aren't you supposed to switch off your cell phone?" he asked.

She turned a cadaverous face toward him, gave him a brief and disapproving appraisal, and then turned away, as if saying to no one in particular, "Don't worry, Pops. They don't care on this airline."

He blanched for a minute, imagining pilot error and a control panel with blinking lights and regular beeps like an EKG ready to flat-line. He could visualize them flying in a gigantic circle at treetop level, skimming over the no-fly zone of the White House and touching off a barrage of ground-to-air missiles or suddenly plunging upside down into the Potomac.

But none of this seemed fated to happen, and so he turned away and resumed where he had left off in his reverie; he continued imagining the various scenarios that might unfold. Florida was nothing new to him; he had visited several times. But as a final destination where he would sink his roots into the thin, sandy soil for a last few years and, maybe, commit himself to someone—that was entirely new and certainly out of character. Todd in Fort Lauderdale and Mort in Sarasota were both good friends whom he knew from New York and Chicago. He could add up the possibilities and virtues of both places and both friends. Each coast of Florida had its reputation and separate microclimate, and each of his friends was in his own way charming, good-looking, and affable. He planned to spend a few days in Lauderdale—Paradise Close, more precisely—in the set-aside gay enclave inside the sunset state, to look at real estate. And then he would drive up the spine of the Florida to Sarasota to visit Mort, who had just retired and bought a small house in a gated community on the south side of the city. Mort had written that there were several interesting possibilities in the area. "An adventure," he commented to himself, enjoying the aptness of the image, "with two different endings but the same denouement."

The remainder of the flight went quickly, and after bounding three or four times on the rough tarmac, the plane slowed and swung toward the waiting exit pod. A shroud of hot, moist air enveloped him momentarily as he exited, before he felt the icy hiss of the air-conditioned terminal. Stumbling around the waiting walkers, wheelchairs, electric people movers, and knots of students texting their safe arrivals to friends back in Washington, he walked along the heavy carpet past kiosks selling souvenirs, romance and mystery novels, and gaudy hats and T-shirts. There were the inevitable Rosetta Stones promising instant and effortless language acquisition and a special *Evangelical Greeting Post* with the picture of a smiling quarterback holding his helmet across his chest in a prayerful gesture. Written beneath the photo was the slogan, "Catch a pass from God; it's the last quarter, and you're a field goal down!"

As they had agreed, Todd was waiting; one of his feet was poised on the serpentine delivery system at the baggage retrieval. He was dressed casually in khaki shorts and a blue shirt decorated with red and green parrots.

"Hey," he said after they hugged. "Which is your bag?"

"Just this," he said, indicating his carry-on.

"Well, then, come on. And welcome to Florida."

"Yes, great, thanks, and thanks for picking me up."

He hadn't seen Todd in over a year, not since they spent two weeks together in Washington. He certainly hadn't changed: he was still dark and handsome, although there was perhaps a more noticeable touch of gray in his black hair and he now had a deep tan.

"We'll take a short tour of Paradise Close before going to the condo," Todd promised as they got to his car. "Very short because there's not much to see. It's a gay city inside Fort Lauderdale. The history once made a good deal of sense, if not the location anymore. About twenty years ago, a group of gay men—pioneers, really—moved into a rundown area full of small houses, which they restored. You know the story: like with Dupont Circle in Washington, first there are gays, and then young married couples price them out. But that probably won't happen here. No young married couples in Florida. There's a small shopping center and bar area and a couple of garden apartments—I live in the nicest one—and several restaurants. But you probably know all that."

They burst out of the parking garage into the blinding Florida sunlight, and after getting the attention of a driver who wasn't distracted by a cell phone conversation, Todd wedged into the long, hesitant line of traffic. There were palm trees planted everywhere in stately geometric rows, as if the tropical foliage were itself part of a larger planned community. They drove past several waterways jammed by massive white yachts and lush rear gardens. Off to the right, about a mile away, was a massive row of apartment buildings and condominiums like bared, jagged teeth jutting up above the unseen blue lip of the ocean. Turning off the main road, they wound through a residential neighborhood and over bright-yellow speed bumps until they passed a sign announcing Paradise Close. From there it was two blocks to the main street. Since it was around noon, the sun blazed overhead, bleaching the sidewalks and streets to a monotonous cement-white color. There were several stores and bars sporting faded rainbow flags that hung limp in the torrential heat. No one was walking on the hot sidewalks, although there was a steady stream of traffic.

"That's my building in front of us," explained Todd, indicating a large, white garden apartment complex. They pulled into a driveway and then swung down into a sunken, open garage to a designated parking spot. Bill hefted his suitcase out of the trunk, and they marched to the elevator, which responded immediately to Todd's key. Rising to the second floor, the elevator doors opened with a thud, and they emerged onto the narrow landing.

The small elevator lobby was garnished with two plastic palm trees colored a lime-green pallor. The carpet was thick with a zigzag pattern of red and blue. It smelled faintly like the entrance to a swimming pool: of chlorine, bleach, and mildew. They walked down the long hallway, dimly lit by yellow sconces, past several apartment doors.

"All this is going," announced Todd, anticipating his reaction. "But not until next year when the association collects a special assessment."

"It's impressive," he lied. "A nice, convenient setup."

Todd opened the door to the apartment, and a rush of light greeted them.

"We'll just set your things inside," he said. "No need to unpack yet. Then we can drive to Stella's for lunch. It's not too far away and not very expensive. Pretty typical of the Paradise scene, too."

They went back down the elevator to Todd's car and then drove out into the glare. The restaurant was only about six blocks away, but without sidewalks except along the shopping strip, going on foot would have been dangerous if not an invitation to sunstroke.

Turning into a small parking lot at the end of the gay area, Todd explained, "There's always valet parking: necessary at night and for the lunchtime rush."

A very good-looking, thin Hispanic man dressed in black shorts and a pink shirt opened Todd's door and took his keys. Todd handed him a five-dollar bill, and they crossed the lot into the screen-porch entranceway of the restaurant. The layout inside was odd, with tables facing onto the parking area and a front open section that looked directly through what must once have been a storefront onto the busy street. In the back corner, there was an inverted L-shaped bar. Around it were chest-high raised tables for drinks or snacks, while booths lined the remaining edges. Several wooden tables and chairs filled the center. Indistinct disco music thumped underneath the rise and fall of muffled voices. About half the tables were occupied by groups of elderly men nodding their gray heads in distracted conversation and looking up for an occasional uninterested survey around the room at the other patrons. Most were heavily built and darkly tanned, their aged skin folding over sagging jaws and belted waistlines. There were a few who wore shorts, sandals, and bright shirts; others sported Palm Beach pastels: pinks, baby blues, and avocado greens. By contrast

Todd looked handsome, dark, and desirable, and a few of the men looked at him with a brief flicker of interest before giving up.

They ordered from the "Light Lunch" section of the menu, which also offered "More Than You Would Ever Eat" and items for those with "Challenged Dietary Needs." Todd asked for a salad, and Bill ordered a BLT. When their food arrived, his huge sandwich balanced precariously over the edges of the plate, and Todd's mounded salad almost spilled onto the table.

"This is a whole side of bacon," Bill exclaimed, looking at the unwieldy layers piled between the slices of the bread and an oozing tomato slice.

"Oh, that's Florida," laughed Todd. "Always too much to eat. Always huge portions. Some of these guys," he said, wagging his fork from side to side at no one in particular, "buy a meal and then take the remainder home for dinner."

"It looks like some of them manage to finish it all in one sitting," Bill said.

"Well, it's true," Todd continued, ignoring the unkind implication but picking up on his point. "What with driving everywhere and lots of lunches and drinks in restaurants, it's hard to stay slim here. Paradise Close is a kind of bear haven, if you can imagine that."

"I wonder how many calories there are in a full serving of boredom," Bill thought, deciding to keep this joke to himself.

"Bill," said Todd. "You'll quickly get used to it."

"It's only that I see myself in all those dilapidated bodies," he explained. "No unkindness intended; I'm just projecting my fears of what I might become."

They finished their meal and then drove back down the Paradise Close strip and headed east toward the ocean.

"Let's go to the beach," said Todd. "I already have towels, suntan oil, and an umbrella in the car."

"Didn't bring my suit," Bill objected.

"Oh, don't worry. We'll go to the nude beach just north of Miami. So you won't need anything anyway."

They drove through several tidy residential streets to avoid the heavy afternoon traffic, passing by carefully manicured lawns and then over several large bridges that gave an elevated view of the Intracoastal Waterway. Emerging onto the beach highway, they quite luckily found a place to park. The sun was very hot, and a steady, stiff breeze blew in off the ocean, rattling the fronds of the palm trees. They crossed the highway and walked to the cement entryway to the beach. There was a three-foot wall along the edge just tall enough to obscure the beach itself from all but the highest SUVs and Hummers. They walked down the sloping dune toward the left, past nude families and couples and into an area occupied only by men.

"It's segregated by choice," said Todd. "You can be nude anywhere along here, and every once in a while, a straight couple or family strays over into the gay section until it dawns on them where they are. I love to watch their reaction, their effort not to show their embarrassment. But you've never seen people pack up so fast!"

They found a spot, and Todd twisted the umbrella pole into the sand and then spread out the towels. After carefully slathering on sunblock, they sat down, Bill in the shadow of the umbrella that was snapping in the wind and Todd fully exposed to the sun. Bill looked around, his regard drawn to the ocean breaking noisily onto the beach. In the jumble of whitecaps, he saw four bathers jumping in the foam, trying to bodysurf over the incoherent waves. Every five feet or so on the beach, a group or couple or single sunbather lay on a towel or in a cut-down folding chair. They were all deeply tanned, and he felt self-conscious about his pale northern body.

"I think the crowd from Stella's has decamped with us to the beach," Bill said. "I don't see anyone under sixty or two hundred and sixty, for that matter."

"That's pretty much Fort Lauderdale," said Todd.

"They look like beached seals…or maybe walruses that have come up onto the sand to mate. Does it bother you?" Bill continued, imagining the largest of them lumbering in the comic gait of an ocean animal thrashing about on its flippers as it tried to negotiate the steep dunes.

"No, not at all," replied Todd. "I think these guys are pretty happy with who they are. Sun, surf, lots of food, friends. Giving up…or into…has its advantages, you know."

"It seems like a slow, bright death to me," Bill replied. "I'm sorry; I don't mean that. It's very personal. I guess I'm afraid to settle down, especially since I'm on the verge of doing so: afraid of what it will mean since it will be my last move."

"Still the butterfly," laughed Todd. "Well, you probably won't find very many open blossoms here—not that your prince exists anywhere. Do you think it's better in Washington, really, at your age?"

"Well," Bill replied, "I keep busy with concerts, plays, galleries, friends. I don't suppose there is much culture here."

"In Miami, of course," replied Todd.

"But what do you do all day? I mean, besides eating, going to the beach, reading e-mail, and the gym."

"That's about it. The day manages to pass quickly."

"I can't believe that's enough for you, Todd. Look around you."

"It is, and I have," replied Todd. "And I think it's you who doesn't understand. For all your culture, what good is it? What's the purpose of satiating yourself secondhand with art? What benefit does it have for you or anyone else? Since you retired and stopped teaching and writing, you're just a presence at someone else's show."

The words hurt, as Todd's frankness sometimes did, but Bill wondered. Did he think he could outrun old age and inevitable decline and forget that he was just a slim and nervous version of the guys who were roasting themselves out on the beach here in Fort Lauderdale? What was the difference? Fat on food or overfed on culture, gluttony is gluttony.

"One compromise is as good as another, I guess," he said.

Maybe Todd was right, he thought. He had never actually added up what it was all for, who benefitted when he went to the opera or a gallery opening.

"So you think I'm just an audience with no one the better for it."

"A consumer, you mean," Todd interjected.

"Yes, that too..." he admitted.

The next few days passed in a pleasant daze of slow-motion, punctuated by meals that were quickly becoming a highlight of the day and brief exposures to the devastating sun. He could feel and see himself gradually browning on the beach and being basted by the sauces at Stella's.

Early on his final Thursday morning after breakfast, he reminded Todd, "I told you I'd be leaving today. I have a rental car reserved, and I mentioned driving up to Sarasota to see Mort. I guess I should get going soon."

"Well, you know you can stay longer with me if you like," replied Todd. "I thought you might look at some places to buy. I can help you find a condo if you still intend to move to Paradise Close. Even in this building. The price will never be better."

"No, I think, for the moment, I'll look at Sarasota. Mort is expecting me today. I just don't know about Fort Lauderdale yet. Perhaps. If it were just you, Todd, you know I'd stay for a long visit; maybe more. But it's me I'm afraid of."

Two hours later, he was in his car speeding up Interstate 95, the mayflies splattering against his windshield like pellets: Florida sleet. He had to stop twice at rest areas to hose off the debris before it hardened into an opaque smear. The air smelled damp and vaguely rotten, and the truncated forest of low palmettos was punctuated only by exits that disappeared into the brush. When he reached the cutoff for Southside, Sarasota, he joined Route 72, a four-lane highway dotted with strip malls that repeated the same sequence every mile or two: a supermarket pawnshop, an oncology center, restaurants advertising "all you can eat and early bird specials before four." The turnoff to Mort's place was immediately after a trailer encampment set back beneath some tall pines. He stopped at the gatehouse, and the young attendant looked up from her iPod to inspect him. She peered disapprovingly at the muck on his windshield but took Mort's letter of invitation without comment.

"Wait until I call him," she said and lazily dialed her intercom. Mort must have answered quickly because the gate suddenly jerked up. "Take Marshall Field Parkway straight past Louis Sullivan Avenue to Pinkerton Lane and turn right. It's the second house on the left. If you reach Palmer Street, you've gone too far."

He passed slowly through the gate and across two speed bumps into this bright little Chicago South annex. On either side of the road were clusters of four or five houses, each grouped around a small pond. In the median of the parkway, short, recently planted and staked palm trees stood motionless in the still late-afternoon sun. He found Mort's driveway and turned in. Mort was waiting at the open door and came out as soon as he appeared.

"Come in, come in," he shouted. "It's really steamy outside but a lot cooler in here. Welcome to Graceland."

Bill grabbed his suitcase from the trunk and walked quickly up the gleaming tile sidewalk to the porch. It was clear that Mort wasn't much of a gardener: a few lonely, fern-shaped palms were set in a yard of shimmering white and beige gravel. Mort hugged him and pulled him inside.

"It's hot today," he said. "But then it always is. I noticed you looking at the yard. I had my choice of styles: 'no care,' 'minimal effort,' and 'green thumb.' You can see which one I chose," he laughed.

"Don't blame you," Bill exclaimed, savoring the first welcome wave of air-conditioning.

Mort pulled the door closed, which gave off the sound of a hatch shutting. "I'll give you a quick tour," he said. "This is the kitchen, small because I don't use it much. I could have gotten the 'Master Chef' model, but the 'Snack Maker' is perfectly adequate for me," he said, opening a closet door to reveal a small kitchen alcove. "Bathroom with Italian tile; then my bedroom," he said, pulling open a sliding door to reveal a large, darkened room filled with heavy wooden furniture and a king-size bed with a heavy red brocade spread.

"And down the hall here," he continued, "the living room, and beyond it the lanai room that looks out onto the water. My favorite place."

The living room was tiled and bright with a huge black television screen at one side and a red leather upholstered couch facing it. There was a low table placed in front with several long black remote devices arranged in precise parallels, two armchairs, and another small table with a fake tiffany lamp. Along two of the walls and above the couch hung brightly colored paintings: large swirling compositions that reminded Bill of the shirts he had seen in Fort Lauderdale. A small bookshelf held magazines and a dictionary.

"We'll go out to the lanai room tonight when it cools down a bit and then have breakfast there tomorrow."

"Lanai room?" Bill queried.

"Yes, it's really a Florida sunroom, but the property management wants us to call it a lanai, after the Hawaiian Islands, because it looks out over the water. So I just fell into the habit. Everyone does."

"That pond, you mean?" said Bill. "Are there any fish? Can you swim? Have you got alligators?"

"Nothing alive, actually. The management puts poison down every so often for mosquitoes. And then they skim off the scum. That why it looks so clean and fresh and tidy."

The next morning he was dozing slightly in half sleep, conscious of the early light cutting sharply through a crack like a spotlight where the dark curtains did not quite meet. Outside, he heard muffled voices and the squeak and shuffle of sneakers on cement in front of the house. Curious, he got up and peered out just in time to see the tail end of a group of fast walkers striding by, swinging their arms vigorously. There were thirty or so that he could see, mostly women in pastel shorts and T-shirts and the odd man or two mixed into the pack. They were chanting something indistinct, but he could only make out a number or two. What were they counting?

128

Later during breakfast in the lanai room, he asked Mort, "Don't you get up to join the exercise group?"

"Yes, usually I do. It a good way to meet people, and it's the only time you can really be outside and not bake in the sun."

Bill frowned and then said, changing the subject, "I have to ask, Mort: are there any other gay men in the community? I've seen lots of elderly women, but…"

"No," said Mort. "I'm by myself here. But then Sarasota doesn't have much of a scene anyway. That's not why I retired here. I just like living in Florida; anything is better than those terrible Chicago winters and the endless, dark, windy spring days waiting for summer. I love it here."

"But don't you miss gay life?"

"Well, there's the Internet, and there's a gay beach of sorts near Sarasota. We can go there later if you want. And there's even a cruising area behind the dunes in a pinewoods where guys drive around in their cars to hook up. You don't even have to get out," replied Mort.

"Bumper sex?" Bill asked and then said seriously, "It sounds like you've given up."

"Not given up at all," said Mort. "Just shutting down gradually. It's a relief in a way. The percentage of hits and misses isn't very much in my favor these days."

"So what do you do all day," Bill asked, "besides shopping and driving around?"

"Well, there are some interesting restaurants in Sarasota, a museum, a couple of galleries, a multiplex movie theater. But somehow the day manages to pass quickly."

As they sat, a slight breeze roiled up by the sun filtered into the room from the open window, carrying sounds echoing from one of the other lanai rooms across the pond.

"One spade…one no trump," he heard.

Mort noted his attention and said, "Bridge starts early here; it's pretty much an all-day affair. I sometimes play myself because there's always the need for an odd man out…so many widows. Most of them are really charming. And so many of them come from Chicago—almost the whole community. I even knew a couple of their husbands before they passed. That's where the name of our community comes from, by the way: Graceland Memorial Park in Chicago,

129

not Nashville of course. So many great names and monuments: Potter and Bertha Palmer, John Peter Altgeld, Mies van der Rohe. They all ended up there."

Bill gave Mort a calculating look. He was still very handsome: thin with brown hair highlighted by age and sharply etched features. His face was often stern, rigidly placid, and immobile, but when he smiled or laughed, a completely different aspect passed over it, causing it to become softer, more fluid, and animated. If he stayed, he wondered which Mort he would see in the morning or when he visited again or if he actually decided to move to Sarasota. He realized, of course, that this was just speculation because he was certain he would go back to Washington; he assured himself he would not move to Florida yet. Perhaps he was, as Todd had accused him, too much of a cultural glutton. But he also felt that this judgment was terribly wrong and that there was much more left to his life than being a passive consumer of someone else's accomplishments. In his quieter moments when he got back, he would figure out what was missing from that stark caricature of his life. He would try to convince himself that being the member of an audience was a legitimate existence in itself for a while longer or at least better than living a sunny death. He refused to equate both realities: home in Washington or here in Florida. He refused to believe that all the choices he would make about the future and where to live were just different versions of the same slow closing down of the senses, weakening of the will, and dissipation of energy. For the moment, Sarasota and Fort Lauderdale seemed very real, vivid warnings of who he would inevitably become. But was he ready to accept that yet? Smiling to himself, he thought of his return encounter with Esprit Airlines. Even the indignities and humiliations of air travel couldn't daunt his sudden high spirits; in fact, they were almost welcome. Nor, for that matter, did the prospects of the next inevitable visit worry him. Next time, he assured himself, he would start out on a different airline. At least there was that.

www.ingramcontent.com/pod-product-compliance
Lightning Source LLC
Chambersburg PA
CBHW060623130626
46555CB00002B/631